"The moment has come, Perdita."

The sound of her name, uttered in that detached, slightly gravelly voice, did strange things to her nerves, but she sat like a statue, staring ahead.

"Perdita? We're going to have to get some things straight." He sat beside her on the bed. She could feel his nearness. "We're about to undertake a most difficult human task—a man and a woman living together."

"We're not living together!" she snapped, though she knew it was inevitable.

"Then what do you call it?" he asked softly, his voice like velvet. "You won't move out. And I *am* moving in."

Perdy couldn't answer. The air between them was throbbing with something more primal than a disagreement about a house.

Bethany Campbell, an English major, teacher and textbook consultant, calls her writing world her "hidey-hole," that marvelous place where true love always wins out. Her hobbies include writing poetry and thinking about that little scar on Harrison Ford's chin. She laughingly admits that her husband, a comedy writer and American TV show host, approves of the first one only.

Books by Bethany Campbell

HARLEQUIN ROMANCE
2726—AFTER THE STARS FALL
2779—ONLY A WOMAN

These books may be available at your local bookseller.

Don't miss any of our special offers. Write to us at the following address for information on our newest releases.

Harlequin Reader Service
901 Fuhrmann Blvd., P.O. Box 1397, Buffalo, NY 14240
Canadian address: P.O. Box 603,
Fort Erie, Ont. L2A 9Z9

A Thousand Roses

Bethany Campbell

To Ruth Pearson,
who helped make Lovematch a reality

Harlequin Books

TORONTO • NEW YORK • LONDON
AMSTERDAM • PARIS • SYDNEY • HAMBURG
STOCKHOLM • ATHENS • TOKYO • MILAN

ISBN 0-373-02803-2

Harlequin Romance first edition December 1986

To Jan Precure,
who knows that certain houses are magic.

CHAPTER ONE

SHE HATED TO SEE A GROWN MAN CRY. But crying seemed to be exactly what Sam Puckett was going to do. His seamed face became contorted, and his scraggly mustache twisted as if he were tasting something bitter.

Perdita sat cross-legged on the gold carpet in her nearly bare living room. She looked up at him in disbelief. He was sitting in the only remaining chair, a gold-upholstered antique.

"What?" It was all she could say. She blinked her dark eyes twice. *"What?"*

"The deal's fallen through," Sam repeated. His mustache quivered like the whiskers of a frightened mouse. "I can't deal with these people any longer, Perdita. Your house isn't going to sell."

"Not going to sell!" Perdita wailed. "But my furniture! It's already on its way to Indiana!"

She felt like weeping but, as usual when she was disturbed, she opted for something more dramatic. She stretched out on her stomach and put her head in her hands. Then she began to beat the carpet with her fists. She moaned. "Perdy," Esmeralda used to say, "you sometimes have a tendency to be altogether too theatrical."

She moaned again.

"Perdita?" Sam's thick New Hampshire accent made her name come out puh-dee-tur. "Are you all right?"

She stopped beating her fists and lay there a moment, staring at the carpet, her mind racing. Of course she wasn't all right. She was lying on the floor of her unsold house in New Hampshire, while most of her furniture was on a moving van headed for Cloverdale, Indiana. And if the house wasn't sold, she couldn't buy her fabric shop in Cloverdale, so there wasn't any reason for her furniture to be going there.

Drat! Sam had warned her not to be so hasty, but Perdy had been sure, for once in her life, that things would go smoothly. Now she'd be stuck in this grim New England winter with an empty house that she could no longer afford to keep. She thought briefly of walking down to the pond, hacking a hole in the ice big enough to fit her body through, and...

Rats, Perdy thought, and sat up, crossing her legs again. That wasn't the answer.

"I'd feel much better if you didn't look so sad," she muttered, wrapping her arms around her long legs. "All right. What did old Ebenezer Scrooge do this time?"

"Squires," Sam corrected her. "Ebenezer Squires." Sam had an uncanny knack for never getting a joke. "Perdita, I'm sorry, but the man is crazy. And his lawyer, that Algernon, is even crazier. Yes, Algernon's the one. He's been nothing but trouble from the beginning. Why Squires thinks he needs a lawyer to buy a house is beyond me. It's Massachusetts thinking for you, that's what. Nobody trusts anybody down there, so everybody has to get a legal eagle. I'm sorry, Perdita, but Algernon claims there's a cloud on the title of the house, and Squires won't buy till it's cleared up."

"A cloud on the title?" Perdy ran her fingers through her short dark hair, frowning. She had a vision of a small surly thunderhead hovering over a legal document, shooting out ominous little lightning bolts.

"First of all, the fool claimed you don't even own the land the house sits on."

Perdy's brown eyes widened and her stomach gave a frightened little flip. "Don't own the land? You mean it's sitting on somebody else's ground, for heaven's sake?"

"No, no, no," Sam said impatiently. "I told you—the man's impossible. Of course you own the land. I can prove it six different ways—none of which he'll listen to. There's no problem at all—except this little bitty one. Look."

He undid the straps of his battered Puckett Real Estate briefcase, then took out a blue and white surveyor's map and spread it on the carpet in front of her.

"See this little corner of the property that's shaded in? It's called a gore area. Right here." He tapped the small pie-shaped area with his silver pen. "There was a small error when the property was sold thirty years ago, before the house was even built. But it's yours. I don't question it. No bank has ever questioned it, or any real-estate company. Believe me, Perdita, the property's been sold six times since then, and nobody's ever questioned it. Until that hotshot Boston lawyer came around—him and that Squires. Massachusetts! It should fall into the sea!"

Sam continued his diatribe, trying to explain the intricacies of title transfers, but Perdy only stared at the map without comprehension. All her plans were dashed by that small blue triangle. Gore area. It sounded like something out of a horror novel: *Its relentless darkness will suck you in. Beware. Slimy monsters lurk fiendishly in the backyard, oozing and burbling*. And all the while, Perdy thought, her furniture was wending its way expensively to Indiana.

"I'm going to lose my shop in Cloverdale then, right, Sam?" She wanted to cry, but habit and willpower held back the tears and kept her voice even, almost light. Perdita had long ago perfected the art of hiding her true feelings. She had been forced to, to survive.

"Now you don't know that, Perdita," Sam said consolingly. "I'll find you another buyer. A sane one. There's been something funny about this Squires and his lawyer from the

start. But don't you worry. I'll get your house sold for you.
I'll call the agent in Cloverdale and explain there's been a
slight delay."

He reached down and patted her hand awkwardly.

"That'd be a lie, Sam," she said, looking him straight in
the eye. "The deal isn't delayed. It's off. I'm going to lose
the shop in Cloverdale."

Sam's mustache began to make its timorous-mouse
movement again. "Look, dear," he began, making Perdy
wonder irrelevantly why New Englanders called everyone
dear, "maybe even that would be for the best," he went on.
Perdy groaned inwardly, knowing the lecture was coming
again. "Honestly, Perdita, you saw Cloverdale, Indiana,
only once in your life—and you just want to up and move
there? I worry about you, I really do. I mean, why do you
want to go to a town you don't even know? Buy a shop
you've never even seen? You told me you don't know anything about business. This whole thing is too impulsive. You
could get yourself in big trouble. Maybe this'll give you time
to think it over, dear. What do you say?"

She wanted to say: *I don't know what else to do. I haven't
got anyplace else to go.* Instead she shrugged and tried to
smile. There was no use explaining her dreams about Cloverdale to Sam, hardheaded old Yankee that he was.

She'd been through Cloverdale once when she was sixteen years old, and although she had an affinity for the
Midwest in general, she felt the need of a more specific place
to call home, her hometown. She'd fallen in love with
Cloverdale on sight: the green lawns, the big white Victorian houses along the main street, the peonies and lilacs
growing in the front yards. Even the dandelions had looked
beautiful to her.

Cloverdale. The name was perfect. It sounded like a
hometown, it looked like a hometown, it felt like a hometown. It was the kind of place she had always imagined.

Sometimes, when she was registering at a new school and had to fill in her birthplace on the entrance forms, she had been tempted to write in Cloverdale, Indiana. Sometimes she scribbled the words in the margin of her notebook. If anybody bothered to ask her where she was from, she sometimes answered, "Cloverdale." It didn't seem like a lie. In her heart, it was home.

As for her desire to own a fabric shop, her reasons for that would sound just as crazy to Sam. She knew nothing about business and nothing about the particular shop, but she knew a lot about sewing. And she knew she wanted to be in Cloverdale. Soon after she had moved into the house she'd inherited from Esmeralda, she had put it up for sale. She knew Esmeralda would have understood. She then had Sam call the real-estate agency in Cloverdale to find her a fabric shop. There would be one for sale. She knew it, just as she had known Cloverdale was home when she saw it. She had been right.

But now she was going to lose the shop. Somebody else would buy it. She knew that, too, with clairvoyant certainty.

Persnickety old Ebenezer Squires and his equally persnickety lawyer had ruined everything. Ebenezer Scrooge, she corrected herself. Christmas was next week, and she'd had that same premonitory quiver of nervousness when she'd heard that her buyer had that horrid, creaking name Ebenezer.

The lawyer had haughtily informed Sam that the buyer was "a bachelor gentleman from Boston who insists on being in the house by Christmas." Even if the papers weren't settled by then, old Scrooge still had to be in the house for the holiday. He insisted he be allowed to rent the house before the sale was final. Sam told Perdy that such rent agreements were common and drew up a contract of such complexity that Perdy's head had ached reading it. She finally signed without fully understanding it.

She had formed a vision of Ebenezer Squires as a sallow, wizened, hunchbacked old man with untidy yellow-white hair, a hooked nose and a jutting toothless jaw. He would wear a pince-nez, and his watery little eyes would squint at the world in sheer malice. If she ever met the repellent old geezer, she'd tell him a few things he'd never heard in bluenose Boston. His withered ears would burn, and finally, maddened by the vituperation of her verbal attack, he would clutch his sunken bony chest and die before her very eyes.

"Perdy," Esmeralda used to say, "you are sometimes altogether too vindictive in your imaginings."

Sam was grumbling, his teeth clenched. "We couldn't deal with those people, Perdita. That lawyer had the unmitigated gall to call this beautiful state Cow Hampshire! This! God's country! And to ask how the hicks up here ran business the way we did! I told him to stick to chasing ambulances, and he called me a name I won't even repeat to you. I can get you a better buyer than these...these villains. You'll see, dear. That lawyer and his stupid rent agreement are a sheer nuisance."

Oh, no, Perdy thought, letting the word *rent* sink into her brain. "He can't hold me to that rent agreement, can he? I mean, now that he's not buying the house?"

"Certainly not!" Sam stuck out his rather insubstantial chin and stood up. "I've got that all down in black and white. No sale, no rental. Those people are crazy, Perdita. We're better off without them. Trust me."

She had little choice, she thought gloomily, watching him struggle into a voluminous overcoat, then don a fur cap with dangling earflaps and an enormous muffler.

Perdy stood up to see him to the door. At five-foot-nine, she found herself at eye level with the top of Sam's cap. Her height had never made her uncomfortable, though. "Stand up straight, darling," Esmeralda had always told her. "Stand proud."

Dear Esmeralda, thought Perdy. And who better could have argued the case for height? For Esmeralda had been tiny, a midget in fact, and she had been like a mother to Perdy. It had been Esmeralda who had willed her this pretty house in the New Hampshire woods, something secure for "my tall girl," as she'd liked to call Perdy. Something solid.

Oh, Esmeralda, Perdy thought, *I miss you.* She felt tears threaten, but she held them back, and watched Sam fumble his way into a pair of mittens that resembled bear paws.

He said goodbye and told her once again not to worry. Perdy nodded dutifully, then closed the door behind him.

She went back into the living room and stared out the big bay window, watching him trundle through the deep snow to his car. Miracle Mountain, the highest peak in the area, loomed in the distance, its stony crest glistening with snow, the pine trees on its rugged sides almost black against the frosty drifts.

"All right," she said aloud to herself, "what now?"

She looked around the bare living room. Only Esmeralda's old armchair was left. Tomorrow the Salvation Army truck was coming to pick it up, along with a few other pieces. She'd have to phone them and cancel.

She sat down in the chair and pulled her long legs up, encircling them with her arms. First, she thought, she would have a good cry. A good, long, snuffling weep over Cloverdale and her beautiful shop—which she would probably never own now.

No, she told herself firmly. Esmeralda would hate her for crying. Her ghost would probably come back and rattle chains all over the place. Neck chains. Wrist chains. Esmeralda had loved jewelry.

"So I'm a little person," she used to say, laughing up at Perdy. "All the more reason to wear big jewels, kiddo!"

None of Esmeralda's jewelry had been expensive, but she'd worn it like a queen, for in spite of her size she had been a beautiful woman.

She had also been a strong one. "When things get tough," she always told Perdy, "you just get tougher. What would your father think if he saw you crying? You'd break his heart."

Perdy had loved her father dearly, and hurting him was something she would never have done. As long as he lived, she'd protected him just as Esmeralda had protected her husband, Frankie. Women, Esmeralda had taught her, had to be the strong ones.

Perdy hugged her legs tighter and stared out the bay window at Miracle Mountain. She would not cry. She'd just sit for a moment and try to think. She stared at the already failing light, cursing Ebenezer Squires and his lawyer in particular, and New England in general, a place so old and respectable and established it scared her. How she yearned to be back in the Midwest.

She was suffering the nagging sense of inadequacy that often plagued Midwesterners new in the East. To New Englanders, any place west of Boston was considered a wilderness bereft of culture. At least, that was how many a bewildered Midwesterner was made to feel.

Perdy had always thought of Yankees simply as the Northerners in the War Between the States. But now she was in the bastion of the true Yankees, the original Yankees, the only people who still called themselves Yankees and were as proud as punch of it. They glowed over such phrases as "Yankee ingenuity" and "Yankee wit." Everywhere she went she saw this pride of heritage, and sometimes Perdy felt as if she were in a foreign country, one in which she would always be an outsider.

She uncoiled herself from the chair and pulled her black sweatshirt printed with large green pandas down past her slim hips. She was a slender young woman; not beautiful, but striking. Esmeralda had taught her how to make the most of herself: how to make up her dark eyes, how to wear her unruly dark hair short and sleek on the sides, with curly bangs in front. And, of course, the million admonitions to stand tall. "All the way up, Perdy—and hold that pretty head high."

"I'm scared," she had once admitted to Esmeralda, when she had resisted starting at yet another new school.

"Honey," Esmeralda had consoled her, "most people are scared a lot of the time. The trick is never to act scared. Just watch your father and Frankie. They're scared, but they don't act it. That's the key."

Perdy took Esmeralda's advice and made it work for herself. She had to. It was a way of protecting herself from all the cruel comments people made about the way she and Frankie and Esmeralda lived. And about the way they looked. A shy girl, she was able to cultivate just enough false bravado to keep any potential tormentors off balance. She stood tall and she developed a crooked little smile that was both cynical and provocative, and a talent for fast comebacks. At least people thought twice before they said anything cruel.

Perdy's father, Nels Nordstrand, had been a professional wrestler on the Midwestern circuit. So had Esmeralda's husband, Frankie, once, when midget wrestlers were an American craze; but the craze and Frankie's back gave out about the same time. He became Nels's manager, as well as the manager of a small shifting cast of other wrestlers with such names as Ravishing Ricky, Hugo the Horrible and the Python Brothers.

Perdy's father was the fixed star in Frankie's ever-shifting realm. Nels Nordstrand was the Norwegian Monster: the Ugliest Man in the World. That was one of the reasons Perdy could never bear to hurt him. Life had already done too much of that.

Nels had not always been the Ugliest Man in the World. He had been a stunningly handsome young man and had wrestled as the Black Viking. Perdy could still remember him, a hero, striding toward the ring in his sparkling black and silver cape. He was strikingly fair of skin, with dark hair and eyes.

In the rowdy world of wrestling, he had been one of the good guys: lean, clean, muscular, and as handsome as a young Norse god. Men had envied him, women had loved him, and children had adored him.

A car accident had wiped all that out in a few fiery moments. Perdy's mother, a quiet, dark-haired woman whom Perdy remembered vaguely as always humming and smelling like cinnamon and meadow grass, was killed instantly. Her father, when he finally was able to leave the hospital, no longer looked like a Norse god. His face was so grossly scarred it was hardly recognizable. His arms and chest hadn't fared much better.

Frankie and Esmeralda, like tiny, fairy godparents, had taken Perdy in. They had never been able to have children of their own, and she became as much their child as Nels's.

It had been Esmeralda who had helped Perdy through the series of upheavals and shocks. She had somehow prepared Perdy, who was only six, to see her father without bandages for the first time and not blink in surprise or horror, but to walk right up to him and kiss his ravaged cheek.

It was Frankie who had convinced Nels that the world had not ended—that he had to go on because Perdy needed him and loved him. Frankie often struck people as a laughable little figure in his pinstripe suit and a cigar that always seemed too big for him. But although he was not always taken seriously, he was a shrewd psychologist.

"Nels," Frankie had said, "you can let this destroy you, or you can use it. So maybe you're not so pretty anymore— so what? The world loves a good villain, too. Think about it. And think about that little girl of yours, seeing you ashamed, a quitter."

It took Nels a long time to pull out of it, and by then both he and Perdy were living with Frankie and Esmeralda. The four of them bought a big trailer, and they followed the gaudy wrestling circuit through the Midwest. Nels began his career again—this time as the Ugliest Man in the World. Wrestling had never been considered very respectable in the United States and at the time was in a slump. Still, they managed to make a living, with Nels wrestling at county fairs and in any town that had a place big enough to set up a ring.

The four of them lived like Gypsies, for Frankie kept them more on the move than ever, convinced that success was just another state away. His small size put him at a disadvantage in the business world, but his dreams were big. Esmeralda always believed in them. "Take Frankie's dreams from him and you might as well kill him," she used to say.

Perdy, always "the new kid in town," had been teased unmercifully—about her father, about Frankie and Esmeralda, about the big old rusting trailer. Adolescence had been one long hell, but Esmeralda, who gave both Frankie and Nels the courage to keep going, kept Perdy going, too.

"We may not be the average all-American family, but never forget how much we love you. Don't you worry what people think—it's what's inside a person that counts. People who say mean things are people with ugliness inside them. Don't pay them any mind."

Perdy knew it was true. But still the teasing hurt, and she developed a kind of wall around her emotions, a facade she never let down except at home. She kept boys at a distance; she'd learned swiftly that they thought her background guaranteed she was wild. Besides, she spent so much of her time with adults, the boys all seemed like silly children.

When Perdy was eighteen and had just finished high school, Frankie died. Once again, Perdy saw what Esmeralda was made of.

She gave Frankie the biggest funeral she could afford, with a full-size silver casket and banks of red roses. She sat through the whole thing with her spine like an iron rod, and because she didn't want anybody feeling sorry for her, she never shed a tear.

Afterward, back in the trailer, she had said, "Would you believe the little squirt provided for me and never said a word all these years? Thirty thousand dollars in life insurance. No wonder we lived on beans half the time! Now why would he do a thing like that?"

Esmeralda's chin quivered, but still she didn't cry. "Well, I gave him some funeral, didn't I? Ever see so many wrestlers in street clothes in your life? He got put away in style, like he would have wanted. That stupid undertaker wanted to put him in a child's casket. Can you beat that? I told him he had a man-size heart, and inside Frankie was a bigger man than he'd ever be. You put him in a full-size casket. Period."

"Esmeralda, what you gonna do now?" Nels had asked in his slow way. Perdy was already starting to worry about him. He had taken so much physical punishment in the ring that his reflexes were slowing and his speech was slurred.

"Well," said Esmeralda, "I guess maybe I'll go home, kids. I suppose that was what Frankie wanted for me. I've been homesick for about a million years. And I'd like to see a couple more New England autumns before I clock out."

"Homesick?" Perdy had blinked in surprise. She knew, of course, that Esmeralda, the daughter of French-Canadian immigrants, had grown up in New Hampshire. But Esmeralda had never, ever, in all the years Perdy had known her, said one word about being homesick.

"Yeah," Esmeralda had said, stubbing out a cigarette. "I still got a little bit of family left up there. A cousin or two. Once a Yankee, always a Yankee, I guess. If I hadn't been so crazy about Frankie, living in the flatlands would have driven me smack out of my head. Yep. It's time for the old girl to go home."

But what about us? Perdy had wanted to cry out selfishly. *What about me?* Esmeralda, her gamin-cut silver hair twinkling in the lamplight, spun one of the big artificial jewels on her tiny hand, and as usual, had seemed to read Perdy's mind.

"Life keeps going on, kiddo," she'd muttered, not meeting Perdy's eyes. "You get yourself to college. You happen to have a very good brain in that pretty head. The way you've always got your nose in a book? The way you can draw and make designs? You get yourself someplace they can teach you to use all you've got. You make something of yourself. You hear me?"

Perdy had nodded numbly. There was no money for college, and her grades, after all the years of wandering, were not good enough for a scholarship.

"Here," Esmeralda said, reaching out for her purse and opening it. "This will get you started."

She handed Perdy a check for two thousand dollars.

"I can't take this," Perdy gasped. "This is money Frankie meant for you!"

"Wrong, sweet thing. He meant it for you. He saved it for you. We both knew our tall girl was going to need some college money some day. So there's a start."

"Yeah, Perdita," Nels said. "I got a little put away for you, too. Esmeralda's right. It's time for you to move on. Make something of yourself. Not like me."

Her father's scarred and battered face had looked so vulnerable that Perdy hadn't been able to stop the tears that time. "I want to be just like you both!" she sobbed. She knew an emotional display would make Esmeralda cry too, so she rushed off to her bedroom and wept into her pillow for most of the night. She wanted to get all the tears out of her system so there wouldn't be any left to upset Esmeralda when she climbed on the plane headed for that distant and foreign place, New England.

About a year after Esmeralda left, Nels became seriously ill. That had been two years ago. Perdy was in the middle of her second year of fashion design when her father's linger-

ing lung illness required that the two of them go on a quix-
otic tour of the Southwest to search for drier, more
breathable air.

For eighteen months the quest went on, with Nels growing more frighteningly weak and dependent on her. Perdy
had learned her lesson from Esmeralda well. She kept her
chin up and her spirits seemingly high. Nels loved it when
she made him laugh. If things went wrong, she always had
a quip to make him smile. She lived to keep him happy and
was terrified of losing him.

They traded the trailer for a van, and Perdy worked a
dozen different jobs in a dozen different cities: in the alter-
ations department of a department store, as a waitress, a file
clerk, even as a costume mistress in a small seedy nightclub
in Las Vegas. During those months she learned more than
ever to keep people at a distance. They had too many questions about the tall young woman and the monstrously
scarred and sick old man Nels had become.

It was in Elko, Nevada, that Nels finally collapsed. They
had been moving a lot and the weaker Nels got, the more
restless he became, as if he were trying to outrun fate.
Twenty-four hours after the collapse, he went into a coma.
Two weeks later he died. Perdy was in a daze of grief.

For all those months, she had tried to be strong, like Esmeralda, but secretly she had hoped that somehow, someday Nels would get well and they'd settle down in a place like
Cloverdale, in a white house with lilacs and peonies growing in the yard. But it was never to be.

Three months after his death, Perdy learned that Esmeralda had died almost within a week of Nels.

She had tried to call Esmeralda after her father's death,
but her phone always rang and rang, ominously unan-
swered.

Perdy had been working as a costume mistress in Las Vegas when she received a letter from Esmeralda's lawyer. It
had been forwarded three times, and with the prescience

Perdy had learned to trust, she knew before she opened it what it contained.

It was a professionally cool letter informing Perdy that Esmeralda had left her her house, furnishings, jewelry and small bank balance.

There was also a sealed letter from Esmeralda, the handwriting spidery and weak.

Dearest Perdy,

Your letters are getting few and far between, kiddo. I hope that's not because there's more bad news. Well, you stay strong, my tall, beautiful girl.

My own news isn't so good. You know that we little people don't usually live to be old people. My doctor says my ticker wants to stop ticking.

I want you to know that it doesn't scare me one bit. I've had so much in my life: Frankie, Nels and you—especially you. And I even got to come home at the end and see those New England autumns again.

Perdy, I know things haven't been going well for you and Nels, but don't worry. I'm going to see you're taken care of. After all, you're the daughter Frankie and I always wanted, right?

I want you to know that a day doesn't go by that I don't think of my brown-eyed girl. You'll like New Hampshire, Perdy. And you need a home after all this time. Nels, too. And you're going to have one.

Love you, love you, love you,
and remember—
Stand Up Tall!
—Esmeralda

Perdy felt sad remembering the letter, and vaguely traitorous for selling Esmeralda's house. But what did a wrestler's daughter have to do with prim and proper New England? It was no place for a person with her background. For three months now, Perdy had felt like a circus zebra at a horse show. She had to get out of New England—go home. But she had no home—except for Cloverdale. Cloverdale had been her imaginary haven for so long that it seemed only logical to go there now. The desire had become an obsession with her lately, one that kept her from going mad with grief.

No, Sam Puckett would never understand that obsession. Perdy wasn't sure she understood it herself. But she did understand clothing design and fabrics and sewing and the shop in Cloverdale seemed like the magical answer to everything. But now it had been jerked from her grasp at the last minute by the so-called gentleman from Boston and his demanding lawyer.

She reached for the phone, which sat forlornly on the carpet in front of the empty fireplace. She had to call the moving company. She was going to have to talk faster than Frankie and Esmeralda combined to get her things back. Impetuously, she had sent her furniture to be stored until she got to Cloverdale to find an apartment. She would have to cancel the storage, too.

Before she could touch the phone, however, it rang.

Who on earth . . . ? She knew nobody in New Hampshire except Sam Puckett, and he had just left. She picked up the receiver as if it were a poisonous snake.

"Yes?" she said hesitantly.

"Miss Perdita Nordstrand?" a harsh gravelly voice asked.

"Speaking."

"This is Arnold Algernon, Miss Nordstrand. I am Mr. Squires's attorney. We have to talk."

She stiffened in apprehension. She sat down on the floor, crossing her legs and wiggling her toes in the furry mukluks furiously, wondering what he wanted.

"I don't think I'm supposed to talk to you, Mr. Algernon," she said carefully. "You're supposed to talk to my realtor. That's why I have him."

"Your realtor," the voice rasped, "is a nincompoop and he's got you into a very fine fix, young lady. If you have a brain in your head, you'll get an attorney of your own—fast. You have legal problems. Serious ones."

Perdy bristled. "And you have a manners problem—a serious one," she retorted, drawing on years of study of Esmeralda in the fine art of backing down opponents. "I want to use my phone, so let's just say goodbye and hang up now!"

There, she thought with satisfaction. That ought to make him think twice about trying to intimidate her.

"That," the voice hissed, "is exactly the kind of rudeness I have come to expect from you small-town, small-minded people. Mr. Squires is a very respectable gentleman from a very fine Boston family, and never—I repeat—never, has he had to put up with the kind of incompetence we have discovered here. We have been shown a total lack of breeding. I, personally, would rather deal with a pack of baboons."

Furious, Perdy decided to bang the phone down so loudly Algernon's ear would ring for a month. But his next words stopped her short.

"Are you prepared to vacate your house so that Mr. Squires may rent it, as agreed upon and signed?"

Perdy drew in her breath sharply.

"Did you hear my question, Miss Nordstrand?"

Slowly she released her breath, feeling dizzy.

"I can't rent my house. I haven't got anyplace to go!" she replied in disbelief.

"I told you we must talk. And I told you that you need a lawyer. I am coming to see you, Miss Nordstrand."

"You are most certainly not!" she countered angrily. She looked around the room rather wildly. "If you come here I'll—I'll hit you over the head with a chair. A big one!"

"In which case you'll need a lawyer even more," the evil voice croaked. "We shall be there in twenty minutes. Good day."

The line went dead.

"The beast!" she shouted in pure frustration. No wonder Sam Puckett had lost patience. Be here in twenty minutes, would he? She could almost hear Esmeralda's throaty little voice: "The trick is never to act scared. Stand up to the suckers with all the moxie you've got, kiddo." All right, thought Perdy, tugging at her dark bangs. All right, you overbearing Boston barrister. You come right over, because you are going to meet the most bodacious female who ever set a spike heel in the sovereign state of New Hampshire. You don't know with whom you are dealing. I was raised by Frankie and Esmeralda and the Norwegian Monster. Watch out, Mr. Algernon!

She stamped upstairs to her nearly empty bedroom and rummaged through the closet. The movers hadn't taken her clothing. She had made most of it herself and would trust it to no one. She would take it with her in the van when—and if—she sold the house.

She flung her tights and long black sweatshirt with the green panda bears onto the old bed and donned her most outrageous creation: a pair of bright-crimson silky lounging pajamas. The top was bat-wing-sleeved, with a sash that tied around the hips. It had a plunging neckline and was printed all over with black silhouettes of little pitchfork-wielding devils.

She put on gold high-heeled sandals and wound Esmeralda's favorite bracelet—a golden mesh snake with jeweled red eyes—around her wrist. Then she marched to the bathroom and added a little more eye makeup. She'd been using more and more makeup since Nels had died, like a sort of mask to protect her from the world.

She went back down the stairs and sat in the gold chair to wait. The fast-falling twilight had almost veiled Miracle

Mountain. She crossed her long legs and tapped the toe of her gold sandal against the carpet. She fumed.

When the doorbell rang she flipped on the hall light and pranced through the entryway to the front door, standing tall, as Esmeralda would have wanted. Her high heels made her an even six feet, and she flung open the door, knowing that she would be staring down at Arnold Algernon.

She was right. He was a short, bloated little man, somewhere between forty and fifty, with a large nose nipped red by the cold and a peculiar-looking hat pulled ineffectually down to protect his meaty ears.

"Miss Nordstrand?" he said, looking up and blinking in surprise.

She stared down at him coldly.

"You, I assume, are Mr. Algernon," she said with all the disdain she was capable of.

"Perdy," Esmeralda used to say, "I sometimes think you are capable of far too much disdain. Cool it."

Arnold Algernon nodded, his eyes fixed on Perdy's cleavage, which was at exactly his eye level.

"I have one thing to say to you," she flung out haughtily. "If Mr. Ebenezer Squires isn't going to buy my house, he is certainly not going to rent it. If he tries to move in, I'm afraid he'll find himself living with me. Because I am not moving out. How do you think he'd like that?"

Arnold Algernon seemed to bloat even more with rage, which made him look toadlike and venomous.

"I think I might like it just fine," said another voice, not quite as grating as Algernon's. It was a velvety gravel, and cold—cold as the New England night. "And if I ever hear you call me Ebenezer again, I'll strangle you. The name is Ben Squires."

The voice jolted through her, and her imperious confidence fled like a leaf in the wind. In spite of her high heels, she found herself looking up at the man standing behind Algernon. In the dim light that fell through the open door

she could see he was very tall, at least six-foot-three. He
wore a shearling coat that hugged a pair of broad shoulders. His dark hair was uncovered, and in the shadowy light,
he looked like a Norse god. Although his words had
sounded half-joking, his face was as hard as New Hampshire granite. Perdy's first thought was that this man was
stronger than she was. The idea struck her like a blow, and
it frightened her.

"May we come in, Miss Nordstrand?" Algernon croaked
irritably.

But Perdy's gaze was fixed on the dark eyes of the man
behind him. She had one of her sudden, visceral premoni-
tions that something was about to happen.

She should have slammed the door in their faces. She
should have told them to stand out there until they froze.
But the tall man knew that he was in total control—was used
to being in control. So instead, she nodded numbly and let
them come into her house.

But she kept standing tall, the way she had always been
taught.

CHAPTER TWO

PERDY LED THEM SILENTLY through the entryway and into the barren living room.

Get a hold of yourself, she scolded inwardly. *So Squires isn't a wizened old coot with humps and wrinkles. But he's just a man like any other. The thing to do is to get the upper hand and keep it.*

Even so, Perdy had a funny tickling feeling in the pit of her stomach and was altogether too conscious of the tall, humorless-looking man behind her. Life, as Frankie had often said, was just like wrestling, and intimidation was the name of the game. If Ben Squires had momentarily acquired the advantage, then her job was to get that advantage back and keep it.

She sat down in the gold chair as if she were High Empress of the Eastern Seaboard and appraised the two men who now stood before the bay window.

Algernon looked angry—but uncomfortable. That was good. His little pale blue eyes were glancing about the empty room uneasily.

But Ben Squires was another story. He hadn't blinked an eye. He just stood there, his dark eyes studying her as coldly as she had studied him, as easy and arrogant as if this were already his house.

He wasn't really that good-looking, she decided. His face was too lean, too severe; his cheekbones were too high, his nose too long for true handsomeness, and, despite his broad shoulders, he seemed to have no hips at all. He was the kind of man Esmeralda had always called snake-hipped, although his well-fitted black slacks left no doubt that his long legs were all muscle.

Under the unbuttoned shearling coat, he wore a conservative gray sweater that revealed with almost studied casualness a white collar and the knot of a black silk tie. As he took off his black leather gloves he looked every inch the proper Bostonian.

Except, Perdy thought, her mind racing, except for that face. The deep grooves on either side of his lean mouth hadn't been formed by smiling. And the way his lips were clamped tight, as if he was holding back some ferocious inner turbulence, was disturbing. They seemed bred to express the same hauteur that Perdy was struggling so hard to project.

His eyes, under dark brows as straight as arrows, were just as disturbing. They were not simply brown, like Perdy's. They were black, and they seemed to say very directly, "I know who I am and what I want. And what I want, I get. Always."

Perdy had seen that look before. Mr. Kim, the manager of the Killer from Korea, had once told Perdy, "It's in the eyes. You can tell a person of iron will from the eyes."

"What about my eyes?" Perdy had asked Mr. Kim. She had been only fifteen, but she'd made her nearsighted eyes hold fast to his unreadable ones.

"Yes," he'd said softly. "You are very young, but it's there. You could fight to the end. But remember, Perdita, fighting is not always the answer."

She had watched men's eyes ever since. Mr. Kim had been right. In a few people, a very few, there was a strange power in the eyes. Her father had had it once, then lost it. Mr. Kim had it, and so did an old retired wrestler she once knew, a man of great gentleness and dignity.

But this man, this Ben Squires, standing there carefully slapping his black gloves against his open palm, had more will than she'd ever seen before, and it scared her. She was going to have to reach deep down inside herself in order to stand up to him.

Algernon's unpleasant rasp broke into her thoughts. "Isn't there someplace we could all sit?" he asked, his eyes rolling about the room like blue marbles, coming to rest on Perdy's long legs, then flicking away again.

"If you want to sit, sit on the floor," she said, haughty as a peacock. "Consider yourself lucky that I ask you to sit at all. I didn't invite you here."

"I refuse to sit on the floor," Algernon sputtered. "It is beneath my dignity. And you might offer to take our coats. The heat in here is smothering."

"I like it hot," Perdy snapped. She draped her crimson-covered arm over the back of the chair. "And I didn't ask you to take your coat off, because I'm not asking you to stay."

Flinging her legs easily over the arm of the chair, she gave him her special stare, the one that always scared men off. Algernon looked at her legs, then her plunging neckline, then at Ben Squires.

Squires's lean mouth curled at one corner. "It's still the lady's house, Algie. For a few more days. Don't worry about inconsequentials. Get on with business, can't you?"

Algernon's pouchy face became redder. "Simple courtesy is not an inconsequential," he argued. "I will not be toyed with by this young—" his eyes finally settled on Perdy's cleavage as if he'd found the word he was searching for "—this young strumpet."

Perdy's eyes narrowed. She wasn't about to be insulted in her own house. But Ben Squires, seeing her anger, smiled coldly, then somehow reduced Algernon's insult to nothing. "Algie, I pay you to make things easier, not more difficult. Just get to work, will you?"

Oh, he was a high-handed one, all right, Perdy thought. He had a sneer fit for a king. She glared first at Algernon, then at him.

But Ben Squires only turned and stared moodily out the window into the darkness, toward Miracle Mountain. After a moment he shrugged and turned around again. He sat casually on the sill of the bay window, crossing his long legs and folding his arms across his broad chest.

Algernon had crouched on the floor in an angry, untidy lump, his hat beside him, his scarf trailing, his overcoat unbuttoned and his woolen mittens stuffed awkwardly into the pockets. He was struggling with a bulging briefcase.

"My, my, Mr. Algernon," Perdy observed, smiling thinly. "If you can't manage to open a briefcase, however do you think you'll manage to move me out of here?"

"I've had enough from your uppity realtor. And young lady, I've just about had enough from you! I'll have you out of this house, all right—you can go live in a snowbank for all I care." He shook a pudgy finger up at her. His efforts to look ferocious and dignified as he squatted on the carpet, still wrestling to unsnap his briefcase, struck Perdy as ludicrous.

She yawned lavishly. "Ho hum," she said, unimpressed. She was beginning to suspect Algernon was totally incompetent, and she wasn't going to worry about his threats. It was Squires who had her worried. He was lounging there watching her and Algernon as if they were a semi-amusing circus act. Why had a man like Squires retained a rude bumbler like Algernon?

"Do you see these papers?" Algernon was demanding. He was on his feet again, the now opened briefcase lying like a gutted kill next to his galoshes. He brandished a fistful of documents in her face.

Perdy refused to answer. Of course she could see them. She might wear contact lenses, but she wasn't blind.

"Do you see these papers?" he repeated. "Do you remember Sam Puckett bringing you these papers? Do you remember signing these papers, Miss Nordstrand?"

Perdy nonchalantly inspected her fingernails, found an imaginary speck on one and flicked it away.

"In case you don't remember," Algernon said, working himself into a high and righteous fury, "you did sign these papers, and you did agree to rent the house to Mr. Squires prior to his purchase of it, and to relinquish it by this weekend! If you do not honor that agreement, I will have you ejected, if necessary, by enforcers of the law!"

Enforcers of the law indeed, she thought. She remembered once when a wrestler named Mean Bull Mahoney had falsely accused Frankie of withholding money from him. He had stormed into the trailer, all three hundred pounds of him, hoping to bully Esmeralda. He roared about calling the police, but tiny Esmeralda reduced the huge man to repentant tears before she was through. Perdy drew on one of Esmeralda's favorite lines.

"Yip, yip, yip," she said in a bored voice, then cast Algernon a dismissive look.

"What's that supposed to mean?" Algernon demanded, his jowls quivering. "Yip, yip, yip? Just what is that supposed to mean, young lady?"

Perdy went on inspecting her nails. "It means, the dogs may bark, but the caravan passes by. Don't threaten me—and don't yell at me."

She'd seen and heard men yell all her life. It didn't frighten her in the slightest. Wrestlers always yelled. They were expected to shout and stamp and jump up and down in fury.

"I'll yell if it's the only way I can make you listen!" Algernon yelled. "You signed this rental agreement! It's legal! You have to rent this house to my client."

"I only had to rent the house to Mr. Scrooge here if he was going to buy it. And he's not going to buy it. Mr.

Puckett said so. Ergo, I don't have to rent it to him. Therefore and to wit, stop shouting and go away. You know where the door is. Head for it. You and Mr. Scrooge both. You're beginning to make me very angry."

"It's Squires, not Scrooge!" thundered Algernon in his best courtroom voice. "And you'd better stop being so flippant! I insist you get a lawyer to straighten out this mess, and very quickly, too."

Ben Squires uncrossed his long legs and put his hands into the pockets of his jacket. "Don't shout at the lady, Algie. It doesn't work. Give me the papers. I think you'd better wait in the car. I can practically hear your blood pressure rising."

Algernon turned to face him, still ready to thunder and rant. "Ben, this woman will not listen to reason. She—"

Squires's black eyes drilled implacably into the lawyer's. "Algie—the car," he said curtly, pointing to the door.

"But, Ben—"

"The car." Squires's voice grated coolly, an edge of disgust in his tone.

Algernon stood for a moment in mute beseechment. Then he handed Squires the papers, picked up his briefcase, shut it and left, as obediently as a well-trained dog. He didn't even slam the door.

Oh dear, Perdy thought. She didn't like the scene now at all. Algernon's presence had provided a buffer between her and her real opponent. She still had the spooky conviction that Ben Squires was somehow dangerous, and being alone with him gave her a funny feeling in the pit of her stomach.

Algernon had slipped away so dutifully she had almost felt sorry for him. What a pair they were. No wonder Sam Puckett had said they were impossible.

"Does your attorney always insult everyone?" Perdy asked, meeting those stony eyes. "Or are Sam and I getting special treatment?"

Light gleamed on his high cheekbones, lost itself in the blackness of his eyes. He leaned back against the window-sill, looking bored.

"Do you always lounge around like the barbarian princess in a sci-fi movie? I'm surprised you don't have six-foot Nubians on either side of you."

Perdy suddenly felt too flamboyant, possibly even gaudy. This hard, lean-faced man was the essence of everything that made her feel uncomfortable in New England. She was disconcerted by his absolute confidence, by his air of superiority that, Perdy had no doubt, sprang from generations of power, money and impeccable breeding, from a world so distant and foreign to her own that she couldn't help being intimidated.

But she didn't allow her gaze to falter. She crossed her arms over her chest and said, "I sent the slaves out to get their swords sharpened. They may be back any minute. So say whatever you have to say and then join your friend."

"Do you want to read these papers, Miss Nordstrand?" He held them toward her mockingly, but didn't move from the window. Perdy would have sat in the gold chair forever rather than rise and take them from him.

"No. I know what they say. No sale, no rental."

"Precisely." His mouth quirked in that cynical half-smile again. "I'm pleased to know you can read. But . . . the sale doesn't have to be void. I want this house, Miss Nordstrand, no matter how well Algie and Sam Puckett have managed to turn things into chaos. I want to be in this house by Christmas. I want to buy it."

Perdy's conflicting emotions crowded together uneasily. His insult about her ability to read rankled, but he looked serious. Maybe he really did want to buy the house. Maybe she would get to Cloverdale after all. And buy her shop, and be in it by the time the peonies and lilacs were in bloom.

She removed her legs from the arm of the chair and placed her feet carefully on the floor, sitting very straight.

"You still want to buy the house?" she asked cautiously.

"Yes. I do. And all you have to do is get the cloud off the title."

"Sam says there really isn't a cloud at all. He says it's some silly thing called a gore area that nobody needs to worry about—that it's no problem at all."

Ben Squires studied her carefully.

"The gore area *is* a problem, Miss Nordstrand. It means that ownership of that section of property can be disputed. It would be very bad business for me to invest in this house when such a situation exists. Algie's making a fuss, Miss Nordstrand, but he's right. Your realtor and your bank should have noticed the problem. And you should have, too, when you bought the house."

"I didn't buy it," she defended herself. "I inherited it."

"Then whoever left it to you should have had more sense," he snapped. "There are right ways and wrong ways to do things. Your benefactor wasn't very astute."

Perdy bridled. Insulting her was one thing, but insulting Esmeralda was another. Nobody insulted her family and got away with it. "Keep my benefactor out of this, you—you Harvard hotshot, or I'll bat you back to Boston like a baseball."

"Yale, not Harvard," he said dispassionately, "and Johns Hopkins. And don't make cheap threats of physical violence. You sound like a gun moll in a bad gangster picture."

"I don't make cheap threats," Perdy shot back, stung by his superiority. "All my threats are expensive. Ignore them and you'll find out just how expensive."

"Surely," he said, "you are not seriously suggesting you'd try physical violence on me?" His voice was calm and mocking, and his light scorn cut like a razor.

She glared at him. "Well, now," she drawled, trying to match both his calm and his scorn, "who knows how far I might go if I got fired up enough?"

"Who indeed?" His voice had a purr that was profoundly insulting. "Your passions seem just as colorful as your—outfit."

They glowered at each other until Squires finally shook his head in distraction and ran his fingers through the expertly barbered dark hair that fell across his forehead.

He sighed, a sound of both weariness and contempt. "Let's get this conversation off the physical plane and onto the economic one where it belongs. First off, where's your furniture?"

Perdy blinked and looked at her watch wildly. Her furniture! Where was it by now? Probably halfway across the state of New York. She'd lost track of time, and it was now well after five o'clock. She couldn't call to stop the truck until tomorrow.

"My furniture, thanks to you, is on its way to Indiana," she said. "I was going to have it stored until I got there, which, also thanks to you, may be never. Which means I'll probably have to pay to have it shipped back here, once again—thanks to you."

"You sent your furniture before the house was actually sold?" He smiled in cool amusement. "That was hardly wise, was it?"

She didn't need to be told that. Piqued, she crossed her arms more tightly. He looked at her and shook his head again.

"Look," he said at last, turning to stare out the window into the darkness that now cloaked the mountain, "do you want to sell this place or not?"

Perdy watched him and was annoyingly aware of the breadth of his shoulders, the narrowness of his hips. She hated his maddening air of all-powerfulness, his patronizing tone.

"Of course I want to sell it."

"And I want to buy it. I also want to rent it. It's imperative I be here by—that I be living in this house next week. As agreed. All you have to do is clear up the business about the gore area."

"And how am I supposed to do that?" Perdy asked. "By magic?"

He turned to face her, and again the cold black of his eyes under those severe brows gave her a jolt. "By taking Algie's advice and getting a lawyer. Algie's a difficult man, and trouble makes him feel important. But he's given you two pieces of good advice. First, the gore area is a nasty problem that should have been cleared up years ago. Second, to do that, you'll need a lawyer, a good one. I'll be glad to recommend one. From Boston of course."

Perdy set her jaw and thought hard. She tapped the toe of her sandal against the carpet and looked Ben Squires up and down—from his dark eyes to his black loafers. He did precisely the same thing to her, his relentless gaze moving from the top of her curly bangs to the golden straps of her shoes, then back again to her face.

"And if I clear up the business of the gore area..." she began at last.

"I buy the house," he replied, putting his hands in his pockets again. "And I rent until the closing papers are signed. I stay here, you go to Indiana. Algie and Sam Puckett will never have to see each other again. We shall all be as happy as clams."

She nibbled at her lower lip. She sensed a catch. "And what if," she asked slowly, "I can't do anything about the gore area?"

"Simple." He bit off the word as if it applied not only to the situation, but to her mind as well. "Then I don't buy the house. And because the banks around here will catch on quickly, nobody else will buy it either. You'd be stuck."

"Wait a minute." Perdy rose from the chair in one fluid movement and stood before him, hands on her slim hips. It was rather disconcerting to have to stare so far up at a man, but she hoped she was doing a good job of it.

"Let me get this straight," she demanded, cocking her head to one side. "I'm supposed to rent my house to you, because you agreed to buy it only on the condition you could rent it until the sale was final."

"Very good," he said slowly and sarcastically. He seemed to be inspecting with amusement the tiny black devils that danced across the front of her blouse. She tried to ignore his gaze and rubbed her hands together, looking down at her nails thoughtfully.

"But if I can't clear up the business about the gore area, you won't buy the house. But you'd still be living in it."

"Correct again. Your perspicacity overwhelms. You see, I sincerely want this house."

"Well," Perdy retorted, putting her hands back on her hips, "where am I supposed to live? And what about my furniture?"

"That," he said, lifting his dark brows in mock good humor, "is not of the slightest concern to me. Rent a place yourself."

"With what?" she demanded. "If I don't sell this house, I won't have any money! I had everything budgeted—practically to the last dime—and now I might be stranded up here with all you—you Yankees!"

"You look as if you're very well taken care of," he said, teeth clenched. "Besides, I'll be paying you rent."

"No, you will not," she replied hotly. "Because you're not moving in here. You and your so-called lawyer—" she jabbed his chest with her finger for emphasis "—are not going to bully me. I don't care how much you threaten, you will not push me around."

"I have a binding legal agreement that says you have to rent to me. And stop stabbing me with that saber you call a fingernail." He hadn't raised his voice, but Perdy could sense his rising anger.

"And I have a binding and legal agreement that says I don't have to move out except for a guaranteed buyer.

Which you are not!'' She poked him in the chest again, hard.

"I told you to stop that," he said very softly, so Perdy poked him again. He made her feel as if she were the new kid in school again, and she hated him for it. She looked up into his smoldering eyes, then gave him a fourth jab for good measure.

He seized her wrist in a vicelike clamp. She blinked in surprise at the pain. "I said," he murmured, bending closer to her, "don't do that."

The surprising strength of his lean hand as it gripped her wrist made her feel vulnerable. She didn't like having him so near. She didn't like the cold black fire in his eyes. She didn't like the intimidating width of his shoulders.

"I am moving in, Miss Nordstrand." He hissed so that Perdy felt like a princess captured by a dragon.

"I'm not moving out, Mr. Squires!" she hissed back, her brown eyes locking with his black ones.

He was breathing hard and so was she. He didn't blink. Nor did she.

Suddenly the situation became intense. The air between them throbbed with something far more primal than a disagreement about a house.

But just when she thought he might put his hands around her throat, he surprised her completely.

He smiled—really smiled—for the first time. He had very white teeth, and his smile was almost wolfish. He took a step back from her, releasing her wrist. He laughed, in one short derisive bark.

"So be it, Miss Nordstrand. I'll move in with you. I think you'll be a most interesting housemate. And it will make a wonderful story to tell at the Yale Club: 'How I lived with the Barbarian Princess'.''

"Don't even think of it," she ordered him, rubbing her wrist. Her cheeks flamed with anger, and she was breathing hard.

He gave another cynical rasp of laughter. "Lord knows I could do with some amusement. Especially at Chris—"

He did not finish whatever he had been going to say. He turned toward the window, staring out at the mountain in the darkness. His mood seemed to change, growing suddenly pensive, remote, unhappy.

Again Perdy was frightened without knowing why, although she knew it had something to do with how close their bodies had been, the hot touch of his hand on her wrist, the way their eyes had challenged one another's.

He turned to face her. He drew on his black leather gloves with a quick, elegant sureness.

"I'll phone you tomorrow to recommend a lawyer," he informed her curtly. Before Perdy could think of a retort he gave her a long, measuring, head-to-toe look. "Sam Puckett says you're going out to Indiana to buy a business. I hope it's not true. Seeing the mess you've managed to get yourself into here, I imagine you'd be a total disaster in business. And—" his eyes rested with cool amusement on the shadowy cleavage revealed by her blouse "—you'd probably lose your pretty red shirt—devils and all."

He cocked an eyebrow and moved to the door. He paused in the small foyer as he opened the door, gazing with disdain at the wreath of pine boughs Perdy had made and tied up with a great bow of crimson velvet.

"That thing," he said with obvious distaste, "has got to go." He shook his head in revulsion.

"Scrooge!" Perdy cried after him. But he had already stepped out into the night, pulling the door shut behind him. "Scrooge!" she called after him anyway. "Bully! Misanthrope! Snob!"

She went back into the living room and looked around, realizing that the worst thing about being in an empty house was that there was nothing to throw.

She flung herself into the gold chair, sprawling like a rag doll that had been angrily tossed. She examined her fingernail, which she had cracked badly when jabbing Ben Squires's hard chest.

"Get a lawyer," he'd said. How could she afford a lawyer? What she'd told Squires was true. She had just enough money to pay the movers, store her furniture and get to Indiana. Except for the house, Esmeralda's inheritance had been a small one. Perdy had to live frugally. She had no funds to spare for a lawyer.

Although she couldn't afford one, she wondered why Ben Squires had hired such a tactless, toadying one. Surely he could afford better. Why, she asked herself, did he want her house so badly? He was obviously wealthy; wealth almost radiated from him. Esmeralda's house was a lovely classical New England house, but he looked like a man who would want something far more expensive. What could he possibly want with a modest and unassuming dwelling tucked into the woods of New Hampshire?

Most puzzling of all, why did he insist on being in it by Christmas? She crossed her legs; those were all good questions, she nodded to herself. She tried, unsuccessfully, to ignore a more puzzling set of questions.

Why, after every damnable thing he had said and done, did she find him so devilishly attractive? She wasn't used to that kind of feeling. The only men she had ever loved were her father and Frankie. Men actually frightened her a bit. Most of the ones she'd met were rough or loud or clearly after one thing. Besides, they needed such terribly good care taken of them, they were a full-time commitment, and she certainly didn't have time for that.

Why, then, when he had been standing there, practically breaking her wrist and staring down at her like some pillaging robber baron, had she felt so peculiar? One part of her had wanted to give him a swift uppercut to his lean jaw, and another part of her went warm and dizzy and funny.

She'd always supposed some day she'd meet a man she'd find attractive—a sweet, gentle, quiet man like her father. But certainly nobody like Ben Squires.

"Perdy," Esmeralda had always said, "I sometimes feel you are altogether too naive. Are you sure you don't want me to tell you more about the birds and the bees?"

Perdy, shy and deeply embarrassed, would shake her head and murmur, "No." The birds and the bees, she had always suspected, were up to no good at all.

CHAPTER THREE

PERDY DECIDED she was having more trouble with Yankees than anybody since Scarlett O'Hara.

Sam Puckett had called the next morning and had been furious when he learned that Ben Squires and Algernon had paid her a visit.

"They got no business bothering you! And you shouldn't talk to them! This is a breach of professional ethics! This is an insult to realtors everywhere! And no, you don't need a lawyer! And no, he can't make you rent to him!"

"What am I going to do about my furniture?" Perdy beseeched him. "I can't pay to have it stored forever—how long is this going to take to clear up? How did I get into this rent predicament in the first place? You told me you were sure the sale was going to go through!"

"Perdita," Sam said wearily, "I said I was ninety-nine-percent sure. Nothing's ever a hundred-percent sure in real estate. You wanted the shop in Cloverdale so bad, and Squires wanted in that house by Christmas so bad, I was only trying to make everybody happy. People make these rent-prior-to-purchase deals all the time. You didn't have to send your furniture ahead. You could have had stored it at this end, until you knew everything was going to go through. I told you that. But no, you had to get to Cloverdale, like it was the Promised Land or something."

"How was I supposed to know?" Perdy lamented. "I've never owned a house before! I've never sold one before—I didn't understand half the things I was signing."

Sam had explained everything again, and she still didn't understand it. She had hung up the phone, chastened.

Perhaps she had been far too headlong, sending the furniture on. But it had never occurred to her that things would go wrong.

Dealing with the moving company had been far worse. Perdy had wanted to crawl through the phone wire and strangle the man on the other end.

"I said," she repeated, "you have to turn the truck around. I don't want my furniture to go to Indiana. I want it back."

"What?" The voice with its thick New England accent was incredulous. "Lady, are you crazy? Once those trucks start moving, they don't turn around. You want your furniture back? Fine. But first it goes to Indiana. You signed a contract. You want it shipped back, then you sign another contract."

"No!" Perdy protested, envisioning her limited funds swirling down a great, dark, endless drain. "You turn that truck around right now!"

"Lady, you signed a contract. If you don't like it, get a lawyer. Goodbye."

Perdy had hung up, wishing she'd never learned to sign her name. Then she would be living happily somewhere, oblivious to the thousand shocks a person selling a home is heir to.

Then the phone had rung, and an irritable voice had begun to fuss at her. It had been a Mr. Dionne from a title company.

"This is to inform you that Mr. Algernon and Mr. Puckett are creating a great deal of trouble for us, although we are working as hard as we possibly can to clear your title."

Perdy had felt like a child being scolded for something she didn't understand.

"Mr. Algernon," the voice went on snippily, "is being very demanding. I just want you to know that this is going to be a long and very expensive business."

Perdy swallowed hard. "How expensive?"

"Thirty dollars an hour," Mr. Dionne said prissily. "And it's going to take hours and hours and hours."

As soon as she'd hung up the phone, it had rung again.

"Perdita?" It was Sam Puckett again, sounding more frustrated than she. "Bad news. I'm sorry. I called the agent in Cloverdale, and he isn't being cooperative at all. They don't like the sound of what's happening here. They're putting the shop back on the market. Today. They claim they have another buyer. Unless you want to pay cash, right now."

"Cash?" Perdy cried in horror. "Where would I get cash? I'm practically stone-broke. All I have is this house and it's trying to kill me! It's like a horror movie! This house is trying to kill me!"

"Perdita—calm down—please!" Sam's voice had sounded almost tearful. "I'm doing all that I can—believe me—but the guy I talked to in Cloverdale is trying to play very tough, very nasty."

Perdy listened to him explain arcane rules of real estate. She was stretched out on her stomach, staring miserably at the gold carpet. How could anybody in Cloverdale be nasty? Cloverdale was home, and everybody there loved one another. It was her own wonderful town where she was going to run her fabric shop. Then someday, a man who looked like a young James Stewart would find her and fall in love with her and shyly propose, and they would live happily ever after.

"The bank thinks you should get a lawyer," Sam was saying. "Don't do it. It's a waste of your money, and this Squires guy has cost you enough already."

He's cost me everything, Perdy thought bitterly: my dreams, my plans, my security, my fortune, my sacred honor, and, most importantly, my sanity.

After Sam hung up, she had dialed the bank, where a man named LeFer had been coldly haughty to her.

Perdy had lost her patience. "Look," she repeated doggedly. "Do I have to rent to Squires or not?"

"That," said LeFer in the chilliest of tones, "is what is clearly ambiguous. It is plainly murky. It is transparently unclear. If I seem to speak in paradoxes, it is because the situation is paradoxical. I suggest you get a lawyer. Fast."

Get a lawyer, get a lawyer, get a lawyer. That was all she'd been hearing lately. She felt as if she were living in an echo chamber.

The phone had rung again. She had recognized the rasping voice immediately. It was Algernon, Ben Squires's lawyer.

"Are you going to be vacating that house, young lady?" he demanded nastily.

"I am most emphatically not," she retorted. "And please get off my phone. Sam says you're supposed to talk to him, not me. This is harassment."

"You'll know the true meaning of harassment when I get through with you," Algernon threatened. "People have tried to fight Ben Squires before, Miss Nordstrand. And they've never won. I repeat—never. Nobody beats Ben Squires."

"Up until now," Perdy had said sweetly and hung up on him. Her head was starting to ache.

She'd then trudged out to get the mail. There were three envelopes for her. She opened the first, an official-looking envelope from the village clerk. She read the notice and groaned. Her state property tax was due—the amount made her wince in pain. She hadn't counted on having to pay it. It was to have been deducted from the final sale agreement. Now they were due. Her head throbbed like a drum.

The second envelope had no return address. She tore it open and took out a note written in a bold, black scrawl. It said: "Here's a list of lawyers. Call one. Call them all if you like. Happy landing!" It was signed "Ben Squires." She crumpled it into a wad and threw it into a corner.

She then opened the third envelope. It was a Christmas card from "All the People Eager to Serve You at Puckett Realty." On the front it said, "Peace on Earth, Good Will Toward Men."

How ironic, thought Perdy as she stood looking out the bay window. It really was Christmastime—and she had never felt more alone or helpless or confused. Her whole life was coming apart at the seams. All because of a tall, dark, cynical stranger who found her situation merely laughable.

She had exactly enough money in her bank account to pay about three-quarters of what she owed. She couldn't afford to rent a place if she wanted to.

Besides, she didn't want to—there was a principle at stake and she wasn't about to back down. Ben Squires had money and power, and he was trying to drive her out of her own house. He was a bully and she was growing to hate him more each hour.

"Joy to the world," she muttered darkly, watching the snow fall. Nobody beat Ben Squires, eh? She'd show him.

PERDY SAT UNCOMFORTABLY in the office of one of the village lawyers. He was a little man, with a little office. His name, appropriately enough, was Mr. Small.

She had on high black boots, a black cape with a scarlet lining, and a dramatic red slouch hat. She looked much bolder than she felt.

Mr. Small had Perdy's papers spread neatly before him on his desk. His fingers were clamped together, and he rested his round little chin on them.

"Tell me the worst," Perdy said, throwing her head back dramatically, as if waiting for him to cut her throat.

Mr. Small regarded her carefully, and he spoke slowly, as if trying to calm some long-legged, exotic and slightly dangerous creature that had invaded his premises.

"Well," he said, "this whole affair is very complicated—Mr. Squires buying from you, and you buying the property in Indiana, contingent upon the sale of your property here. But the worst part of all, of course, is the rental agreement, which is, as the bank stated, ambiguous."

"Oh." It was all she could say.

"Mr. Squires would be renting from you until the sale closed. You, in turn, would go ahead to Indiana to await the final sale of your New Hampshire property."

Perdy nodded, waiting for some revelation that would solve everything simply and neatly. She was afraid it wasn't coming.

"Sam Puckett is a good realtor—he'd have to be, to put together a deal this complex. But I don't know how on earth he let the rental clause slide by him. I don't envy you, my dear, having to go up against Ben Squires. He's become a ruthless man. I'm surprised to see him back here."

Perdy blinked her brown eyes and peered out curiously from beneath the brim of her big hat.

"Back? What do you mean, *back*?"

"Ah," said Mr. Small, sighing. "He used to summer here as a boy. With his uncle, old Dr. Ben Squires. On Miracle Mountain. The place burned down, though, years ago."

She shuddered slightly. Fire had always frightened her; it reminded her of her parents' accident.

Mr. Small was perceptive. "Oh, no one was hurt, my dear. Old Ben was long dead by then. The place was empty.

"I said," he added, "young Ben was ruthless. Well, perhaps relentless is a better word. I suppose he's had to be—so many people's fortunes riding on his shoulders. You've heard of Toynbee's, of course?"

She nodded. Toynbee's was one of the most famous department stores in the United States.

"Ben Squires owns the controlling shares—he also runs it. He's a Toynbee on his mother's side. He was forced to take over management when it was teetering on the edge of bankruptcy. I doubt if most men could have risen to the challenge. He's restored it to its former magnificence, but—he's changed. What happened to him would change most men, I'll wager."

Perdy shuddered again, a more subtle one this time. She'd seen that relentless look in Ben Squires's eyes; that implacable quality, hard and black as onyx. There was something adamant and hungry in his lean face.

"So what about the rental agreement?" she pressed, straining after any crumb of hope, any particle of defense.

Mr. Small gave a little sigh. "On the one hand, it can be construed that he has every right to move in. On the other hand, it can be construed you have every right to remain there. You can stop him by going to court, my dear, but I'm afraid it would be expensive. Yes, very expensive. It's a shame something like this must happen at Christmas."

Perdy sighed. So much for the season to be jolly, she thought as she left Mr. Small's office feeling miserable. She was fifty dollars poorer and no closer to solving her problems.

All she knew was that Ben Squires had her back against the wall. He was trying to force her out of her house, and her money was running out. She needed to get a job.

Well, she thought, setting her chin, after all the months of wandering with Nels in the Southwest, she was an expert at finding jobs. She thanked heaven that New Hampshire had a healthy job economy.

Four hours after leaving Mr. Small's office, Perdy had found gainful employment as a cocktail waitress at Mr. Pongo's Lounge on the outskirts of Manchester, the city closest to Mortimerford, the village in which she lived. She felt momentarily triumphant, but as she drove back to the house, her sense of elation dimmed. Sleet began to drive down from the dark sky, and her old blue van slipped and slid on the crooked mountain roads. She added another item to her list of Things to Spend Money On: snow tires.

"PERDITA, IT'S CRAZY," Sam Puckett told her the next day, "but you're going to have to let him move in. He insists he'll be in there tomorrow. You can come stay with Emma and me. It's the least I can do."

Perdy stood in Sam's office looking at his tired and wrinkled face. He seemed exhausted. He sat at his desk slumped and shrunken.

"He's not chasing me out of my own house," she vowed. "He can send every lawyer in Boston after me, but I'm not going to be forced out." She stood so tall that Esmeralda would have been extra proud. But she was getting frightened.

Sam said that the owners of the Cloverdale property were angry, and that the agent had insisted he had another buyer. Nothing Sam was saying would convince them to hold the shop for Perdy. And nothing he was doing seemed to satisfy Algernon and Ben Squires about the gore area.

Perdy suddenly had the giddy sensation that none of this was really happening. Soon she would wake up, back in the old trailer, and Nels and Frankie and Esmeralda would be there to take care of her. She couldn't really be in this impossible situation. She couldn't.

She still couldn't believe it either, the next day, Saturday, when the men brought in the baby grand piano. Ben Squires, Sam said, was due to move in that afternoon, that very afternoon, but he had a new piano sent first.

Perdy watched, with true horror, as the men tried to struggle through the entryway with the gleaming black piano.

"You're gouging the railing!" she cried. "Stop! Be careful!"

"Lady, we ain't jugglers," one of the three grunted, glowering up at her briefly. "This entrance is narrow. We're doing the best that we can," he said breathlessly as one piano leg knocked a chip off the plaster of the entry wall.

"Stop!" she begged, but they didn't. She imagined herself driving them out of her house with a broom, but after all, there were three of them, and they were piano movers. Even Nels wouldn't have fought those odds.

There were more grunts, more groans, more scratches, more chips, and Perdy finally fled upstairs to her room, lay down on the lumpy bed, and beat on the mattress with her fists in frustration. At least she had a mattress to beat on, she thought.

Perdy felt relieved when she finally heard the moving truck pull away, and decided to venture back downstairs to survey the damage. She was dressed in flowing electric-blue harem pants with a matching top. Its sleeves billowed and it wrapped tightly around her midriff, drawn in at her waist with flowing ends. She had on her gold high-heeled sandals and Esmeralda's snake bracelet. As usual, the more insecure she felt, the more flamboyantly she dressed, to reassure herself.

Lately the amount of eye makeup she wore was directly proportional to the stress she felt. It was as if it, too, could protect her from the bumps and bruises of the world. She had put on enough mascara that morning to give Cleopatra a run for her money.

The piano stood like a big, lustrous hippopotamus in the bay window, and the entryway looked as if a war had been waged through it. Perdy clenched her fists, vowing silently that Ben Squires would pay for every crack, chip, dent and tear.

The movers had left the front door open and she noticed they had even knocked the pine wreath off the door. She stalked to the door and picked up the wreath, straightening its velvet bow. She hung it back up, but it had a slightly drunken look. It made her feel lonely and homesick. She used to make wreaths every year for her family and the families of the other wrestlers Frankie had managed. Nels had always taken her out to collect pine boughs and cones, and Esmeralda had helped her make the bows.

She had just shut the door and was stamping back into the living room when she heard the front door opening.

No, she thought. He can't really be doing it. This can't really be happening. She turned and froze as she watched the door slowly swing open. He wouldn't really do this to me—not at Christmastime.

But Ben Squires stood there, his height and broad shoulders almost filling the doorway. He was hatless, his dark hair falling over his forehead, and he was wearing tight, faded jeans, heavy boots, and a wolfskin parka.

His lean face looked bored and aristocratic. He stamped his feet casually, as if he walked into women's houses unannounced every day.

He glanced at the slightly crushed wreath on the door. "I told you," he said, not bothering to look at her. "This has got to go."

He detached it from its nail and threw it into a snowbank, stepped inside and shut the door firmly. Perdy went nearly faint with anger and disbelief.

"You!" she snarled. She put her hands on her hips. She tilted her chin up and stood straight as a queen.

"And you." His tone was dismissive. His mouth looked grim and his cheekbones were even higher than Perdy remembered. They gave him the look of some dark, Medici prince. But the same black fire was in his deep-set eyes.

"All I can say," she growled, holding her chin even higher, "is you are the most despicable, inconsiderate and overbearing man I've ever met. You are going to pay for every bit of damage your goons inflicted on my entryway when they dragged in that cursed piano. You have turned my life into a living hell. And you'll pay for that, too."

She held her regal pose, hoping her words would crush him like an avalanche of icy boulders.

"And all I can reply," he answered, breaking into his wolfish grin, "is you're the one who insisted on playing house, not me. Now here you are, decked out like my personal slave girl. Shall I ask you to dance for me? Or would you rather peel me a grape?"

"Oh!" she said, her nostrils quivering in distaste. She put her hand to her bosom to indicate she was mortally offended. He cocked a black eyebrow and regarded her hand, and where it was placed, with great interest.

She gave a disgusted sniff and turned her back to him. With all the dignity she could muster, she marched upstairs into her bedroom and slammed the door behind her. She wished it had a lock on it. How dare he accuse her of wanting to play house with him? And how dare those mocking, superior black eyes gaze at her like that?

She sat for a moment on the edge of the lumpy bed, her heart throwing itself against her chest like a panicky deer crashing into an entangling fence.

It is happening. He is really here. He is really moving in. He is really doing it. And he is really handsome, she thought, her mind whirring.

No, no, no, that was irrelevent. He wasn't handsome. He was just imperious and self-contained and so damned male. He was unlike any man she had ever met. Most of the men she had known were wrestlers and promoters—big, beefy men, not lean and hungry-looking like this one. They developed personas that were loud, swaggering, flashy—filled with bluster and primitive emotion. They didn't stare at you coldly, with perfect control, and their words didn't sink into your skin like perfect little Renaissance daggers with poisoned tips.

What was she going to do about him? For that matter, what was she going to do right now, at this moment? She'd made her exit from the living room for the sake of drama, but it hadn't been well planned. She didn't have to go to work for two hours; she couldn't sit in here until then.

Suddenly the doorknob turned, and he was standing there, snake-hipped in his jeans. He had divested himself of his wolfskin coat. His bulky V-neck navy-blue sweater, obviously hand knit, emphasized his broad, square shoulders. Underneath he wore a white oxford-cloth shirt, though, at the top of the V, she could still see some dark hairs curling against the golden skin of his chest. His mouth was clamped in the familiar frightening way.

"Get out of here," she ordered sharply, hoping the best defense was a good offense. "This is my room, you pirate."

The nostrils of his hawklike nose flared. He held out a small rectangular piece of paper.

"I came to pay the rent. Here."

Perdy refused to move. "Put it on the bureau," she said tersely, cocking her head in that direction. The old bureau was the only other piece of furniture in the room.

Immediately after he did so, Perdy realized she'd made a tactical error because now he was in the room. He didn't look ready to leave, either. She could feel his presence as strongly as if he were bombarding her with some sort of rays. The room didn't seem large enough for both of them; then suddenly the whole house didn't seem large enough.

"We have to talk, you know," he finally said, and she refused to meet his gaze. "The moment has come, Perdita."

The sound of her name uttered in that detached, slightly gravelly voice did bizarre things to her nerves, but she sat like a statue, staring straight ahead.

"Perdita."

Again her nerves danced, as if they were filled with tiny, dizzy bees.

"We're going to have to get some things straight." He sat down beside her on the bed. She could feel his nearness. The bees now felt as if they were buzzing in her throat and ears as well.

"We're about to undertake a most difficult human task— a man and a woman living together. I'm sure that you know from experience, as I do, just how complicated that can be."

"We're not living together," she snapped, irritated by his insinuation about her experience.

"Then what do you call it?" he asked softly. His voice was like velvet at her ear. "First of all—" he gave the old bed a disparaging pat. His hand brushed hers, and she jumped as if struck. Steady, she told herself. Very, very steady. She could smell his cologne. It was musk. "This stuff will have to go in the basement. You can sleep in my bed."

She whipped her head around to stare at him in outrage. He gave her that contained half-smile that made his cheekbones seem even more pronounced.

"You vile and odious—" she began, but he cut her off, putting a lean, warm finger to her lips, making them tingle.

"I mean a bed that belongs to me." His finger rested on the fullness of her lips. She raised her hand and pushed it away, then put her fingertips over her tingling mouth. "Not the one I sleep in. I'm having some things shipped from my other place in upstate New York. It's a very nice bed. Antique. Mahogany. About the color of your eyes. And a lot more comfortable than this thing."

He leaned back, resting on his elbows. His shoulder brushed hers.

"This 'thing' is mine, and I'll stay in it," she retorted, edging away from him imperceptibly. "Put your own 'things' in the basement. And leave the color of my eyes out of it. And get off my bed. I don't remember telling you you could lounge on it like a big—lizard."

He didn't move, only stretched out his legs, crossing his booted ankles.

"And we're going to have to do something about the heat," he went on. "It's stifling in here. You, as I remember, like it hot."

His low voice gave the phrase a suggestive little flip. "I paid for the oil, and I'll turn the heat as high as I like," she taunted. "We're practically in the arctic circle up here, and I hate it! I'll make it ninety degrees if I like!"

His black eyes were surveying her as if memorizing her slowly, bit by bit, from the top of her blue blouse to the tips of her gold slippers. "Oh, yes," he said disdainfully. "You came here from Las Vegas, didn't you? That's what Sam Puckett had told me—when everything was a bit more friendly. You don't know how to dress for the cold. That little number might be fine in Saudi Arabia, but here—" he shrugged his wide shoulders as if contemplating her hopeless folly.

"You might do fine in Saudi Arabia," she snapped. "Why don't you go there? I think you'd fit right in with the sheikh set."

"I like it precisely where I am, thank you," he replied, giving her an insincere smile, showing his white teeth. He was so close she could actually feel the heat of his body.

"What were you in Vegas?" he asked softly. "A show girl? And who left you this house—an admirer?" He touched the golden snake bracelet that wound around her wrist.

"I sewed costumes in Las Vegas," she said acidly. "And the woman who raised me left me this house. So don't get the wrong idea, Mr. Squires. Other people have from time to time, and they've regretted it."

"I'm not a man who allows himself regrets," he replied. He leaned over and brushed his lean fingertips against the smooth white skin of the inside of her wrist. "Such white skin," he murmured. "Your arm looks like ivory next to that bracelet."

She rose abruptly, angered at his presumption and at her body for responding to his nearness. "If you won't get out of here, I will," she announced. "I don't have to take this. I'm going for a walk."

He, too, rose swiftly. Before she could go anywhere, he was standing in front of her. He put his warm hands lightly on her upper arms. "But we have things to talk about. The heat. Kitchen privileges. The bathroom. Any number of intimate little things. After all, we are living together, you and I."

She shook his hands off impatiently, but her skin tingled. "Don't touch me you—you Grinch, you," she snarled between set teeth.

"Grinch?" His upper lip curled.

"Haven't you ever heard of *The Grinch Who Stole Christmas*?" she asked, furious, pushing past him and rummaging through her closet. "That's you. The way you push yourself into my house, insulting me at Christmastime—the hardest Christmas of my life, too. You're the essence of Grinchness."

"Christmas," he snapped, still standing by her bed. "Don't tell me you're a sentimentalist on top of everything else. Christmas—ha!"

"Yes, Christmas," she fumed, tossing out her mukluks and jeans from the closet. She had to get out of the house— go for a walk. "Or is your attitude simply the classic *Bah! Humbug*?"

He was silent for a moment, and she kept flinging things from her closet—her tights, a cotton turtleneck, an old sweater.

"Bah, Humbug says it very nicely," he growled at last. Then she heard him leave. She almost felt him leave. Suddenly the room seemed too quiet and very, very empty. She had hit a nerve with him at last. Christmas, was it? He didn't like Christmas. Oh, she'd remember that.

She emerged from her room, bundled in her jeans and mukluks, her layers of sweaters, and her fake-fur jacket and matching cap. She went downstairs and found Ben stretched out in her gold chair, boots crossed, her phone in his lap. He was acting as if he owned the place. He didn't bother to look at her.

"Who said you could use my phone?" she demanded irritably.

He glanced up, a quick scathing glance. His dark brows were stormy. "Don't be childish," he ordered. "I'll pay you back."

"You bet you will," she agreed hotly, but he went on dialing and ignored her. Really, she thought, the man had incredible nerve.

She went through the kitchen and out the sliding doors that led to a small deck, and pulled on her woolen gloves. Her breath rose up before her in a thick plume.

She whistled twice and waited. She wondered if that silly half-stray dog was around today. The woods behind the house glistened with last night's fresh snowfall, and the dark pines were layered with snow like twinkling frosting.

As she started on the path to the pond, she heard the dull rumble of big paws galloping through the snow, then saw Bummer emerge from the darkened woods.

Bummer was a big black dog—part Labrador, she guessed, and possibly part grizzly bear. He had started coming around when she first moved in. She had called the Humane Society to see if anyone had reported a dog missing. The answer was no. So Perdy had half-adopted him. Esmeralda had probably fed him, and Perdy did, too, whenever he showed up.

She called him Bummer because he seemed to be a sort of drifter, just as she was, belonging to no person and no place.

Except, she tried to remind herself, she belonged in Cloverdale. If she could only get to Cloverdale, everything would be fine. If. If it weren't for Ben Squires, she'd be there now.

She walked with Bummer down around the big pond, which was dusted with ice. There was a short dock with a crude diving board, a shed, and a lifeguard's wooden tower, all looking solitary in the snow.

She walked farther along to the foot of Miracle Mountain, down into the valley where, under the bare trees, the brook was iced over in complex layers of silver.

Perhaps she had been wrong, she brooded, inadvertantly kicking some snow with her mukluk. Perhaps she should go further into debt and rent a room. Sharing the house with Ben Squires was going to be impossible. He reminded her of the rich boys in high school; he had taken one look at her and decided she was his for the asking.

But Perdy had always been able to handle them, she reasoned, to set them back on their heels with a few well-chosen words. But Ben Squires was no boy. The worst thing was that some deep, primitive, part of her actually found him attractive. She wished it wasn't true—her life was complicated enough already.

She was still adjusting to the loss of Nels and Esmeralda—her family. The only thing keeping her going was her dream of Cloverdale.

But Esmeralda wouldn't have wanted her to run from Ben. She would have put her little hands on her hips and said, "Give as good as you get, Perdy. You're Nels's daughter and practically ours, and we're fighters. Every last one of us."

Every last one of us. *I am the last one of us,* thought Perdy. *I'm all alone now.* Suddenly she was swept by a wave of homesickness and longing—not for Cloverdale, which seemed almost imaginary—but for the old trailer, for

Frankie and his smelly cigars, for her big, quiet, scarred father, and especially for Esmeralda.

Maybe all this was punishment, Perdy thought darkly—she had a superstitious streak. Esmeralda had wanted to give her a home, to have her keep the house and live in it, to learn to love New England as Esmeralda herself had. Maybe she should never had tried to sell the house. *Esmeralda, are you hurt? Are you angry?* Perdy asked herself as if she were praying. *Esmeralda, what should I do? What can I do?*

But the only answer was the darkening sweep of the wind.

WHEN PERDY RETURNED to the house, Ben Squires was still sitting in her chair, glowering out the window, watching darkness fall over Miracle Mountain.

Perdy hurried upstairs, removed some of her layers of clothing and touched up her makeup. She put her coat and hat back on and raced down the stairs.

Ben hadn't moved. He looked perturbed. "What's wrong?" she gibed, deciding to treat him as she would any man trying to take advantage of her—nastily. "Did you get all depressed with nobody around to pick on?" she jeered, getting her purse and car keys organized.

He gave her a quick, cool glance.

"They misrouted my furniture," he growled, his voice like a vocal thunderstorm. "Idiots!"

"Misrouted it?" she crowed, and tried to keep from laughing. It was about time something had gone wrong for him.

"It's in Baltimore, Maryland," he grumbled.

"Baltimore!" This time Perdy did laugh. "Ha! Well, I may be as poor as a church mouse, but at least I have a bed for the night. Enjoy the floor. And stay out of my blankets. I've got just enough for myself."

He gave her another of his deadly looks, then stood up. She wished he hadn't; she kept forgetting how tall he was. "Where are you going?" he demanded.

What business was it of his, she wondered, and why should he ask in such a peremptory tone?

"To work. Some of us don't loll about on our inherited wealth. Ta-ta."

One lean hand darted out like a snake clenching the dark fur of her jacket sleeve. "And just what kind of work does a girl go to dressed in jeans that tight and wearing all that makeup?" His smile was appraising but cold.

He took a step closer to her, and she felt herself flinching instinctively.

"I wait tables," she bit off. "Disappointed?"

"No," he said. "Disbelieving. Girls who dress like you don't wait tables. Girls who dress like you are always very well taken care of. Very."

She stared up at him in defiance. Something in the way he was looking at her gave her that warm, dizzy feeling inside again. Why? she asked herself irritably. He was just a colder, snobbier version of other men who had tried to take advantage of her, believing she was something she was not.

"You don't know anything at all about girls like me," she said, narrowing her eyes and jerking her arm away. She brushed the fur of her jacket sleeve, as if flicking away the imprint of his touch.

He gave her a slanted, superior smile. "And maybe you don't know anything about men like me. Or about yourself, for that matter. We're both adults. Both alone. In the coldest of seasons. The very coldest. Yet here we are. Together."

She took a small step backward and slung the strap of her purse over her shoulder. She wanted to defuse the tension that had suddenly arisen.

"We're not together," she protested.

He gave her that cool and slightly crooked smile, then looked out the window toward the mountain. Something in his face seemed to darken, to change. "Of course we are.

And you're the one who insisted on staying," he said, displaying his profile. "I came here to be alone."

"I'd rather be alone myself," she said, resisting the desire to swallow very hard. He had a profile like a dark, ferocious hawk, she thought—independent and solitary.

He cast her a brief, contemptuous glance. "Lord," he muttered. "What liars human beings are."

He turned away and stared out toward the darkness, in the direction of the mountain, almost as if he were looking for something. The set of his wide shoulders was vigilant, but proud.

PERDY TRIED not to think of Ben at work. What he had said haunted her: they were both adults, both alone, together in the coldest of seasons. But she did think of him, constantly warning herself against him.

She was tired but vaguely satisfied when she finally returned from work, parking her dented van next to his black BMW in her drive. There might be no Christmas spirit in the house, but Mr. Pongo's Lounge had been bursting with it, and her purse bulged with tips. If the natives of the Granite State stayed as generous as they had been tonight, she just might be able to pay everything she owed.

The house was dark, but she could see a dim, faintly orange light issuing from the bay window as she walked through the snow to the door.

What was that funny light? she wondered as she entered the house. Then she saw a fire in the fireplace, gold flames leaping, and a long dark form stretched before it.

A fire, Perdy thought in alarm. He'd built a fire. She didn't even know if the chimney was safe. She hated fires and had never built one. And, from the look of the fireplace, neither had Esmeralda. Yet, even in her jacket, she could feel the chill in the air. He'd turned the heat down!

She hung her cap on the newel post, then tiptoed to the fireplace. There wasn't even a screen. Sparks could leap out, ignite the carpet, send the whole house up in smoke!

She knelt quietly, and examined the logs and flames. Maybe she should put it out, for safety's sake. Her heart thudded uneasily as she watched the yellow tongues leap, the red embers pulse eerily.

Suddenly a strong hand leaped out, seizing her arm. Perdy lost her balance and found herself curled on her side, her back to the fire, staring at the flame-gilded face of Ben Squires.

He had built himself a sort of nest by the fire, using his wolfskin coat as a pillow. He had one blanket partially draped over him, and his broad chest was bare—golden and shadowed with black hair.

"So you decided to come to me," he said, his voice velvety. His other arm reached over her, holding her fast.

"The fire," she gasped, staring up at him, half-frightened. "I—I don't like fires."

"Fires keep you warm," he muttered huskily, drawing her closer. "Umm. You're cold. You're so deliciously cold. Come here."

She had a glimpse of a golden face lowering itself to hers, and muscled golden shoulders gleaming in the firelight.

She felt his hard, hot mouth nuzzle the edge of her own, press itself with teasing lightness against her still cold cheek, then move slowly, deftly, to her cool lips.

She couldn't resist him. She felt suddenly as if she had been too long without human warmth, human contact, human touch, simple affection. She felt like a person who had been sealed in ice, then suddenly freed, who falls exhausted and desperate into the waiting arms of the rescuer. And she felt something else, too—something new to her, terrifyingly new, yet at the moment irresistible.

She felt the coarse hair of the wolfskin tickling the side of her throat, felt his lean fingers curling and twining in her thick, smooth locks, felt the sheer strength of his arms.

His mouth was firm and still against her own. Then he turned his face slightly, his hand against the back of her head, pressing gently, bringing her face more surely, more intimately to his. Then, with an urgency, his mouth explored hers, tasted hers more deeply. She felt tantalized; a rush of unexpected pleasure coursed through her body. Half-bewitched, she let his coaxing mouth tempt hers to savor his.

The flicker of her response seemed to set him afire, and his kiss became one of power and mastery. She gasped and put out her hand to stop him. She felt stunned, witless, drunken. But inexplicably, her gloved hand was touching his face, shyly exploring the sculpted plane of his cheekbone.

It felt so wonderful to be held, to be warmed, to feel life coursing through her. It was as if she had just come back to life after an endlessly long and cold night of the soul, and the source of life was Ben, irrational as it seemed.

"Your bare hand, Perdita," he whispered against her lips. "Touch me with your bare hand." Then his mouth was on her own, drinking it deeply. She felt the thick silk of his dark forelock mingling with the curls of her bangs, vaguely tickling her forehead, felt the line of his heavy eyelashes against her cheek.

His strong hand was stripping off her glove, placing it against his face, pressing its coldness against the hot, hard curve of his jaw. His other hand was beneath her jacket, pushing up her sweater, exploring the satin smoothness of her back.

"Damn jacket," he muttered, his mouth against her pulsing throat. "Take it off." His lips moved to the vulnerable area just beneath her ear. "Take if off," he ordered again, softly.

Yes, she thought without thinking. Yes, yes, yes. She wanted out of the cumbersome jacket. She wanted to be as close to him as possible, her length pressed to his. She needed to keep feeling that amazing surge of life sweeping through her body.

Her bare hand inched down his face to his neck, then rested with tentative wonder on his naked shoulder.

His shoulder was naked! Startled, her eyes flew open, and she tried to pull away. "No!" she breathed. She snatched her hand away from his shoulder as if its sensually smooth hardness could scald her.

He was staring down at her, unsmiling. His dark eyes were hidden by the shadow. The lines etched beside his mouth looked deeper, crueler in the flickering light. "What's wrong, Perdita?" he said mockingly. "This is what you stayed for, isn't it? And why I let you stay? So this would happen. We both knew it would, from that first night. Let it happen, I mean."

"Nothing's going to happen," she protested raggedly, looking up at the unrelenting lines of his face, the gleam of the firelight dancing on his dark hair. She was breathing fast because she was frightened—frightened that he was right.

He took her hand and held it against the hardness of his chest. She could feel the silky crispness of his hair, the intriguing play of tensing muscles, the strong, drumming beat of his heart.

His other hand touched her face, his thumb warm against her trembling lower lip, stroking it lightly, very lightly.

She lay as still as she could, gathering the shattered fragments of her common sense, her self-respect. He leaned and kissed her first on one wing-shaped eyebrow, then the other. He raised his head, then started to bring his face down against her throat, his other arm winding around her as she arched her body more intimately to his.

"No!" she cried again. She used both hands to push him away. She would not allow him to use her like this—even if, briefly, she had wanted him. For a moment she had harbored the illusion of being loved; but love was not at all what he had in mind.

When he tried to draw her nearer, she surprised him with a swift chop with the edge of her hand across the iron hardness of his upper arm.

She wriggled away from him agilely and leaped to her feet. She stood, almost panting, edging away from him, away from the fire. "No!" she repeated.

He rolled over on his back, looking lazily up from his makeshift pillow of wolfskin. He rubbed his bare bicep, flexing it gingerly. "You know," he said casually, as if nothing had happened, "for a woman, you hit damned hard. Interesting." There was almost a grudging note of admiration in his gravelly voice.

"For a gentleman of Boston, you hit pretty low," she countered angrily. "You had no right to grab me like that."

"You practically crawled into bed with me," he returned. "I don't like teases, Perdita. Don't play games with me."

He put his hands behind his head and looked toward the fire. The light played across the taut muscles of his arms and shoulders.

"Good night, Perdita," he said, dismissing her.

Her anger rose at his gall. "That's one of my blankets," she said contemptuously. "Give it back. I don't intend to freeze tonight."

He yawned, stretched luxuriously, his hands still locked behind his dark head. "Snatch it off me if you want. But I'm buck naked underneath. As for freezing—well, you made your choice. Good night. You can go away now."

"Good night!" She wished she could hurt him as deeply as he had hurt her. She remembered that he hated Christmas and decided to quote a carol. "Sleep in heavenly peace!" she snapped and stalked off to bed, knowing that somehow the words had done the trick.

She could feel his anger, almost the palpable shape of it behind her. It swelled, filling the space of the little house, like the ghost of Christmas past, rattling its chains.

Just what did he hate so much about Christmas? she wondered. Why did he have to be here, in her house, to ruin the holiday for her as well? She had to stay out of his way, she thought apprehensively. He had altogether the wrong idea about her. At least, she thought, touching her tingling lips, she hoped he did.

CHAPTER FOUR

PERDY DID NOT SLEEP in heavenly peace, and she awoke Sunday morning to a hellish racket.

The noise seemed to come right out of the wall. It was an off-key bass voice, slightly hoarse, and loud as a bull moose. It kept chortling the same line from a Gilbert and Sullivan operetta. "I am the very model of a modern major general—"

Oh, Lord, thought Perdy, trying to wrestle more warmth from the blankets. He was in the shower and experimenting with his voice, letting it bounce, reverberate and echo off the tiles. Perdy had done the same thing herself, but not at the crack of dawn. "I am the very *model* of a modern major general—" he sang.

She groaned and rolled over, reaching for the pillow to put over her head. She groped blindly, then realized she had no pillow—it was in Indiana.

"I *am* the very model of a modern major general—"

She could just see him in there, his head thrown back, lathering himself with her soap. In fact, she could imagine him just a bit too clearly, with all those lean, compact muscles.

Guiltily she remembered last night. She had let him kiss her, had even kissed him back—in Esmeralda's living room! Perdy had been brought up very strictly. She imagined Esmeralda staring down at her from heaven, shaking her silver head in disapproval. "Look at you, Perdy," Esmeralda would say. "After all I did to raise you to be a nice girl—and you lie on my living-room floor—with a naked man."

Perdy moaned. Now the naked man was in her shower singing. She had only let him kiss her because she had been tired and lonely and confused. That was all, she assured herself. She might just as easily have picked up a stray cat and cuddled it. Well, she vowed, he wouldn't get through her defenses again. She would be so cold to him from now on that icebergs would come to her for lessons.

"I am the very model of a modern major *general*—"

What was he so cheerful about? Perdy grumbled to herself, especially since it was barely daybreak. She wished the opposing forces would drop a large, modern bomb on the "modern major general."

She uttered a prayer of thanks when the shower was shut off and the singing stopped. She tried to tunnel more snugly into the blankets, finally felt almost warm, and drifted back to sleep.

She woke up again. She didn't know how long she had drowsed, but again the house was filled with a foreign sound. He was playing his damned piano!

Perdy cursed and reached for her robe. Everything was a blur. She didn't have her contacts in and couldn't read her watch. She slipped her horn-rim glasses on, gathered her things and, dull with sleepy wrath, staggered for the bathroom.

"Perdy," Esmeralda always used to say, "you are definitely not a morning person."

Ben had used up most of the hot water. She shivered and winced, enduring a brief, tepid shower, then reached for her towel. He had used her towel, too—the one big, fluffy one she hadn't packed. Some nerve, she fumed, patting herself dry with the limp towel. It gave her a disquieting and forcible sense of intimacy to stand, nude, covered by something that had just been touching his body.

He was still playing the piano, alternating Gilbert and Sullivan with cool jazz while she dressed. She was so angry she shook. It had taken her three tries to get her contacts in right, and then she had nearly blinded herself by sticking her mascara wand into her eye.

He was still hammering away when she marched downstairs into the living room to confront him.

"You used all the hot water! And my towel!" She stamped her foot.

He kept playing, but tossed her a brief, unrevealing glance.

She stood with her hands on her hips, seething. She wore her black tights and a soft, wide-sleeve white wool tunic with a boat neck. It fell just to her knees and was belted with a black cummerbund. Like most of her clothes, it was dramatic, but not at all revealing. So why did she have the uncomfortable feeling that with one short look he had undressed her?

"You," she said, cocking her head. "I am talking to you."

"Ah," he said, giving her his one-sided, mocking smile. "The sleeper awakens."

"You bet the sleeper awakens. How can I help it with you yodeling in the shower like a—a water buffalo? And now this? At daybreak, yet!"

He shrugged and gave her another one-sided smile, then his black gaze fell back to the keys. "Water buffalo don't yodel. And it's almost ten o'clock."

Perdy gave a delicate sniff. "Like I said—daybreak. I happen to work late. And if water buffalo did yodel, they'd sound like you."

She flounced into the kitchen. She knew she couldn't even begin to be coherent until she'd had at least two cups of coffee.

She leaned groggily against the counter. She had left one pot unpacked, and now she stared at it intently, willing the water in it to begin to boil.

Suddenly Ben stopped playing, and she felt, rather than saw him come into the kitchen. She ignored him, but she had a funny tingling in her stomach and at the back of her neck.

"You have a horrible disposition in the morning," he said, as if it gave him untold satisfaction.

"It's because I've had a horrible morning," she said between set teeth.

She gave him a quick, sidelong glance. He was leaning easily against the kitchen wall, his long legs crossed, his hands in the pockets of his faded, tight-fitting jeans. He wore moccasins and a heavy ivory crewneck sweater that set off his bronzed skin, his black hair and dark eyes.

"Maybe we should start over," he suggested, watching her take the instant coffee from the cupboard. "Why don't you say, 'Good morning,' then I'll say, 'Good morning,' and we can both be merry beams of sunshine."

"What makes you so cheerful?" she demanded. She was angry about the shower, angry about the piano, and angriest of all about their encounter the night before in front of the fire.

"Why shouldn't I be cheerful?" He took his hands from his pockets and held them out as if to indicate the beauty of the house around them. "Here I am, exactly where I want to be, exactly when I want to be—and I even get a glamorous little house mouse thrown into the bargain."

"I'm hardly little. And I'm certainly no mouse," she returned sharply. "Go someplace else and be cheerful. I haven't had my coffee, and if I feel like a member of the animal kingdom, it's the pit viper."

"Hmm," he observed. "Just like my little sister. God help her future husband if he speaks to her before she's had her morning fix of caffeine. An indication of low blood sugar, you know."

Ignoring him, she swung open the refrigerator door, then gasped. It was full of what Perdy could only think of as intruding food—food that had invaded her premises. Two shelves of horrible-looking things—carrots and bean sprouts and tofu and yogurt and other such ghastly stuff.

Her own meager stores were huddled forlornly on the top shelf. She took out a stale cream-filled chocolate cupcake and a jar half full of maraschino cherries. It was either that or peanut butter for breakfast, and she wanted to save the peanut butter for lunch.

She made a steaming cup of coffee and leaned against the counter. She wished he'd stop watching her. He looked too sure of himself lounging there, his ebony eyes taking her in as a man might slowly sip a fine wine.

"That," he said as she plucked a cherry from the jar and popped it into her mouth, "is the most disgusting thing I've ever seen in my life." His voice grated with scorn.

"Then you've lived a sheltered life." But the cherry, shriveled, did taste revolting.

"Hardly." He gave that short, rough laugh. "Our food shows the difference between us. I treat my body like a temple. You, on the other hand, treat your body like a pool hall. You should eat more sensibly."

"The difference between you and me," she retorted, "is that you think your money allows you to push around anybody you want. I, on the other hand, come from people who refuse to be intimidated."

"That," he answered dryly, "I am beginning to realize all too well."

Perdy drained her cup and made more coffee. With disturbing certainty she felt that he was undressing her with his eyes again. Her heart was starting to hammer traitorously.

"Do you always put on eye makeup first thing in the morning? And dress like you're going out to pose for *Vogue*?"

"Always," Perdy replied stonily, then ate another cherry. Nels and Frankie and Esmeralda had loved their tall girl to look good—like dynamite in fact—and to dress well. She had always done so for them, and she considered it almost a sacred trust.

"Pity," he growled. "I hoped—just maybe—it was all for my benefit."

"Your benefit?" She nearly choked on a bite of cupcake. It tasted like cardboard.

"You know," he said with a casualness so studied it was intense, "I thought maybe you were inviting me to finish what we started last night."

She stared at him in anger and amazement. What had happened last night had been a mistake; he had momentarily penetrated her armor. It would not happen again. "Dream on!" she said, straightening herself to her full five feet, nine inches.

She tried to control a shiver that went tickling down her spine. For in spite of her resolve, she remembered last night all too well—his strong naked arms, the warm taste of his mouth exploring the innermost secrets of hers. But all that was only physical. She would not make the same mistake twice.

She turned her back to him. She raised her cup to her lips, her hand trembling. She was offended and embarrassed in a way that both perplexed and excited her.

"I did dream on. And on and on and on. It was very nice. And so were you."

He was standing close behind her now. She could feel him there.

"I like your short hair," he whispered. "It shows off that long, lovely throat." Then, with tantalizing lightness, he trailed a fingertip along the nape of her neck, then back. She felt her emotions clanging together like cymbals. She wanted him to stop, yet somehow she didn't. It was as if her body had just declared secession from her mind.

"And your ears. Your white and very delicate ears." His fingertip moved to the silky skin behind her earlobe, sending subtle tremors through her.

Then she felt his lips nuzzling the identical spot behind her other ear. His breath was warm against her throat, and she felt a shuddery weakness overtake her, filling her body with light and heat and sparkles.

His voice was velvety. "Don't tell me you're not made up that way to tempt me again this morning. I won't believe you." His hand caressed her right wrist. "Is that how you got this snake bracelet? As a reward for being such a good temptress?"

His lean hands moved lightly to her shoulders and he kissed the nape of her neck, a slow, gentle, exploratory kiss. She tried to stand very still and very straight, but without thinking she closed her eyes, sucked in her breath. He was making her feel sensations she'd never experienced, completely alarming sensations.

"Perdy! He's playing you like he plays that piano of his!" she could have sworn she heard Esmeralda's voice exclaim, sharp with warning. Yet here Perdy stood, in Esmeralda's house, in spite of all the promises she had made to herself, allowing herself to be seduced, and worse, liking it.

"Perdy!" It was Esmeralda's voice again, and it was alarmed. "Seduction? For shame! What would Nels think? And Frankie? I've told you a million times, kiddo—you go to bed with the man you marry, and that's that!"

Perdy's reaction was immediate, instinctive. With all the force she had, she shot her elbow backward into the hard muscles of his stomach and brought her heel down on his instep with such force she hurt her own foot.

She was deeply satisfied as she heard his startled intake of breath. She wheeled to face him, her eyes blazing with anger.

He was grimacing slightly, his white teeth set, and one lean hand massaged his midsection tentatively.

"My God," he said, his voice tight, his dark brows drawing together in a perplexed frown. "You really do hit hard. Where'd you learn to do that?"

She expected to see anger or icy cynicism in his eyes, but there was something else, an expression she didn't recognize. She was as disgusted with herself as with him, and she glared up at him like an enraged tigress.

"I learned that from my father, Mr. Squires." She remembered Nels, big and scarred, brave, yet frightened of death at the end. "He was a wrestler. I grew up in a tough world, and my father taught me to take care of myself." Her voice shook with emotion.

Ben smiled, a satiric look on his saturnine face. "A wrestler? Oh, good Lord. A profession wrestler? One of those hulks?" he said in amused disbelief.

His reaction was the one she'd heard for years and grown to hate. Of course someone like Ben Squires would think her father a clown and a fool and something very close to a huckster. How could he know what love and gentleness was in the man?

"Yes," she shot back. "A professional wrestler. I imagine you think that's terribly funny. He never went to Yale. He never went to college at all. He couldn't afford to. He made his living the only way he knew how."

"My," he said, raising one straight eyebrow. "You sound defensive. What happened? Did you get teased a lot?"

She drew in her breath. "As a matter of fact, I did. By people just like you. They liked thinking we weren't quite respectable. Well, we were. My family—my family—" She blinked hard, remembering Frankie and his ridiculous cigar and Esmeralda, all fake diamonds and real courage. Ben watched her so closely, it made her uncomfortable.

"My family were fine people," she managed to say, fighting the lump in her throat. "Even if they weren't your kind. They taught me to respect myself and to take care of myself. So stop playing games with me. I'm not going to be your Christmas plaything. Or anybody else's."

She tossed her head back, snatched her coffee cup, and glowered at him.

He folded his arms across his chest and stared down at her. A sardonic smile played across his mouth. His black eyes looked half respectful, half amused.

"Bravo," he said, giving her a curt nod. "If you're so respectable, why are you staying here, at the house? You obviously don't care two cents for your reputation—letting a strange man move in with you. And you certainly haven't gone out of your way to be unattractive. What's a poor, proper Bostonian to think, except that he's dealing with a woman of easy virtue?"

His dark, mocking gaze challenged her, and the grooves etched beside his mouth deepened, as if he were trying to keep from laughing.

"If I cared what people thought," Perdy said, "I'd have killed myself years ago. And I don't care what you think, either—so long as you keep your fat paws to yourself."

He gave a suppressed laugh, unfolded his arms and examined his hands, flexing the long, sensitive fingers. Perdy remembered them moving with deft sureness over the keyboard.

"Ah," he sighed in feigned sadness. "My poor, deprived, maligned, fat paws. Very well, Perdita. I'll keep them to myself. Unless I'm specifically invited to do otherwise."

He stuck his hands in his hip pockets and looked down at her, the corner of his mouth curled slightly. "But if we don't make love, we don't have to go so far as to make war. Would you be willing to negotiate peaceful coexistence?''

She studied him suspiciously.

His eyes held hers. "I'm serious. I'd even offer to shake on it. But see? I'm not even offering you my fat paw. It's tucked safely into my back pocket. But if you want to shake hands and come out not fighting for a change, I'm agreeable."

He seemed serious, despite his smile. "No more using up all the hot water," she said firmly. "Or my towel."

"Agreed. I forgot I didn't have a towel. I'll even take it to the laundromat for you."

"No more singing in the shower or playing that piano when I'm asleep, either."

He nodded amiably.

"I mean it," she said, pointing her finger at him.

"I will be as quiet as a congregation in silent prayer."

She set down her coffee cup and crossed her arms over the breast of her tunic. Esmeralda's snake bracelet glittered on her wrist. "You have to stop being so critical, acting so superior, too," she ordered, chin up. "And I'm going to make a new Christmas wreath and put it up. I am also," she said with great emphasis, "going to have a Christmas tree. I will, if I want to, dress up in an elf suit. This holiday is going to be hard enough without you doing your Scrooge act."

His broad shoulders seemed to stiffen, the light in his eyes sharpen. The crooked smile froze on his face. At last he nodded sharply, like an ax falling. "I won't be critical. For Yale and my country, I will strive to act no more superior than God created me."

He sighed. "As for Christmas, just don't overdo it. Wreath? Fine. Tree? All right, if you must. Elf suit? No, positively. Try—and I know this is going to be hard for you—to be a little understated about the whole thing. Well—at least you can't outdo a department store for Christmas madness with the whole pushy, greedy rush."

He'd made a major concession, and Perdy was surprised. "All right, then," she said grudgingly. "Shake." She offered her hand.

He didn't offer his. "One more thing," he stated, squaring his lean jaw. "The heat. You like it at seventy-five. I like it at sixty-five. I suggest we compromise at seventy degrees, except at night when we turn it down. I went out early this morning and bought my own blanket, so you can have your extra one back."

She withdrew her hand, considering. Her brow furrowed. "I'll agree. But only if you promise to wear pajamas. I don't want to meet you in the hall some morning in your birthday suit."

He laughed. "I don't own pajamas. And if you meet me in my birthday suit, it might help you to wake up faster. But I've got a jogging suit. I'll wear the sweatpants. And we each do our own dishes. Fair enough?"

She thought it was. "Fair enough." She offered him her hand again.

This time he took it, and they shook, a brief and thoroughly businesslike shake. She couldn't help but marvel at the strength in his hand. He had the most beautiful masculine hands she had ever seen. They looked like the lean, powerful hands of a saint in an El Greco painting.

Now what? she wondered. She didn't want to look up and meet his eyes again. There was something different about their relationship now, and she was glad. At least she thought she was glad; but why did she feel unaccountably shy with him all of a sudden?

No, she thought, giving herself a swift mental kick where it hurt most: her conscience. She really couldn't stand him. She simply found him attractive—merely sexually attractive. For the first time, she understood what sexually attractive meant. It meant little gold bees in her nerves. It meant betraying Esmeralda's strict upbringing. It meant trouble.

She turned and stared out the sliding glass doors that led to the deck. The woods stood dark at the edge of the snow-draped lawn. She realized, with a start, that the tumult and warring were over, and she actually was living with a man. What would people think?

"Who cares what people think," Esmeralda always used to say. "You have to do what you think is right."

She hadn't run from the fight. She hadn't let Ben Squires intimidate her. She had held her ground. She even had his promise not to make any more advances. All that was okay, wasn't it? *Was it?* Yes. Let people think what they would. Esmeralda was right. But why, then, did Perdy now feel so strange with Ben? As if she had somehow compromised herself?

"You don't look happy." His low voice sounded mocking again. "Don't you want to be friends, Perdita?"

She didn't want to turn around. She felt as tongue-tied as when she was a gawky teenager in a new school.

"My friends call me Perdy," she said gruffly, still refusing to look at him. She made herself a third cup of coffee and went into the living room. She set the cup down, then went to the hall closet. She grabbed her tote bag full of yarn and returned to the living room, plunking herself down in the gold chair. Ben came into the room and sat on the piano bench facing her, his elbows on his knees, his long fingers knit loosely together.

She rummaged through the yarn bag, picking out the little balls of scrap she wanted, tossing them into her lap, choosing her crochet hook, and began a chain stitch.

"Why so quiet, Perdy?" he asked. "Or is this the real you I'm seeing at last?"

She fumbled and lost a stitch. "I don't know what to say to you, now that we're not fighting," she muttered, recapturing her stitch. "And you keep watching me. It makes me nervous. Why don't you play your piano? Or something."

"You sound as if you've had to do a lot of fighting in your time," he mused.

She refused to look at him. Yes, she thought. She and Esmeralda both had done a lot of fighting—to survive, to win respect, to overcome obstacles, to keep their men going.

"What are you making?" he asked, still watching her. "Winter underwear?"

She lost another stitch. "I'm making Christmas-tree ornaments. I told you I wanted a tree. Esmeralda's ornaments are in Indiana with everything else. In storage."

That storage, she was reminded, was going to cost her a pretty penny, or more accurately, several thousand pretty pennies. She had no idea if or when Sam was ever going to straighten up the business of the gore area. Every time she'd called his office lately, he'd said things were no better.

"Who's Esmeralda?"

"The woman who raised me," Perdy replied shortly. She didn't want to talk to him about Esmeralda. He wouldn't understand about her and Frankie any more than he did about her father. "Why don't you like Christmas, anyway?" she asked, changing the subject. She began to crochet at a furious rate. "Is it the department store? I know you own a department store. Mr. Small told me."

"Ezekiel Small?" Ben's laugh was derisive. "Is that old chatterbox still around? He has been known to tell all he knows. Well, the department store is part of it. It turns into a madhouse every Christmas. It's eleven stories high. Ten are for the store, and the penthouse is for me. You know what it's like having ten stories of Christmas merchandising going on under you? It gives you nightmares."

"With all those cash registers playing 'Jingle Bells'? You should love it. So should your shareholders."

He snorted impatiently. She stole a quick glance at him, her hands still working the hook and yarn. His face looked troubled.

"The shareholders do love it. And most of them are my relatives—more the pity. They like having their stockings stuffed with Christmas profits while I manage a ten-ring circus. Pushing shoppers, griping department managers, worn-out clerks, and triple security guards for the merrily roving bands of yuletide shoplifters, pickpockets—even flashers. Lord!"

"Flashers?" Perdy asked in disbelief.

"Flashers," he replied sourly. "We've got one we call Kris Kringle. Every year he manages to get into the lady's lingerie department, corner a bunch of women, sweep open his trench coat, drop his pants, and yell, 'Ho, ho, ho, ladies! Look what Santa's brought you!'"

"That's terrible," Perdy said, trying not to laugh.

"Laugh if you want. You never had to try to tackle him while he was running off through the Miss Debutante department."

"And you did?"

"I happened to be passing by. I also happened to be a quarterback at Yale, I add in all modestly."

"In a championship season, no doubt," gibed Perdy.

"No. Worst damn season in the history of the school. And the flasher wasn't that hard to tackle. His pants were falling down."

Perdy looked up and stopped her crocheting for a moment, then continued. She couldn't help smiling. "You can't say it's boring."

"No," he said. His tone was light, but she sensed a darkness beneath it. "You can't say it's boring. Toynbee's is a stuffy store—a snobbish store—but at this time of year, it's hardly boring."

"Tell me more," she coaxed. She sensed he hated the Christmas madness a large department store engendered, but he seemed to have come to his own ironic terms with it. He wasn't a man to walk away from a challenge; she wondered if there were some deeper reasons.

He shrugged and told her, with disparaging humor, of the window dressers throwing temper tantrums, the engineering staff going berserk trying to keep the escalators running and the lights burning on two thousand Christmas trees. About the Santa Clauses who were bitten and wet upon by frightened children, the lost children, the maniac who phoned in the bomb threats.

It did not, Perdy decided, sound like a good way to spend Christmas.

"And," he concluded, "there are always a few psychotic episodes. And the accidents. And the people who get sick. And one fatal heart attack."

"Heart attack?" She looked up at him. Something changed in his tone. It was no longer wry or mocking.

"The crowds. The pushing. The heat. The crush. Oh, yes, at least a couple of heart attacks. But always one fatal, it seems. In ten years at Toynbee's I've saved a few victims. I'm glad of that. But I lost one last year. A man keeled over, right at the Christmas decorations counter. I got down from my office long before the ambulance got there. I tried CPR—everything. Nothing worked. By the time the ambulance arrived, I knew I'd lost him. You always hate to lose a patient. Maybe that's another reason I escaped this year."

Perdy stopped crocheting. He was staring at his bronzed fingers, flexing and unflexing them.

She frowned, biting the inside of her lower lip. She uncrossed her long legs. "I don't understand," she said carefully. "You lost a patient? You talk like a doctor."

He looked up. His expression was masked, distant. "I was a doctor. Almost."

"But—"

"No. It's a long story. One I don't talk about." He rose and paced restlessly to the window, looking out at the mountain. He had his hands in his back pockets, and the width of his shoulders contrasted with the narrowness of his hips.

A doctor, she thought, studying him. He had been a doctor? Why was he running a department store? Again she wondered why he was here, why he had to have this particular house, why he so often stared, brooding, at that mountain.

"Let's change the subject, Perdy. And change your clothes too—let's go for a walk. It might be our last chance for a while. Looks like it's going to sleet."

Without protest, she put her things back into the yarn bag. But she didn't get up. She watched him looking out at Miracle Mountain—as if it held some secret that would yield only if he looked long and hard enough.

"Ben?" Her throaty voice was gentler than usual. "Why did you want this house? My house?"

He was silent for a few moments. "Easy," he said at last. "The view. I used to spend a lot of time on that mountain. With my uncle. Uncle Ben. The lovable old village doctor. I wanted to grow up to be just like him."

He turned and faced her. His black eyebrow cocked cynically. "I was a nice fellow in those days, Perdy. Believe it or not. I was even happy. I came back to get to know the mountain again, to try to figure out everything that's happened. Because I'm not a nice fellow any longer. You've seen evidence of that. I'm not a nice fellow at all."

Her brown eyes held his for a moment. Then she rose, nervously, and went to change.

What had happened to him? she wondered. What was hiding behind those cold, unreadable black eyes? Did he disguise his feelings as much as she did? Or did he, perhaps, disguise them even more?

CHAPTER FIVE

"WHAT'S THAT?" Ben asked in mock revulsion. "A charging moose or the Hound of the Baskervilles?"

Bummer was thudding joyously through the snow to join them, his pink tongue lolling, his breath rising like steam.

"That's Bummer. He comes with the house."

Perdy bent and patted the prancing dog, rumpling its black fur.

Ben shrugged more deeply into his wolfskin parka. "Truly the house with everything—even woman and dog. Am I expected to feed this thing when you're gone?"

She straightened and began to walk again. *When she was gone.* For a while she had stopped thinking about leaving. The thought gave her an odd and unexpected pain.

"I suppose," she said carelessly, watching the big dog bound ahead of them.

When they reached the pond, Bummer immediately skidded out on the ice, slipped, and fell unceremoniously on his rear. Perdy laughed, but Ben scowled, then whistled.

"That ice isn't as thick as it looks," he told her. "That's why nobody's skating on it. It'll be another week before it's safe."

Perdy shivered, not just at the thought of the dark, frigid water below the thin ice. The wind blew more sharply and cruelly. The temperature was dropping fast. Her face stung with the cold.

"Who owns all this, anyway?" she asked, gesturing toward the pond, the surrounding woods, the mountain. "Are we trespassing?"

He shook his dark head, his hair tossing in the rising wind. "The village owns it. More precisely, the children of the village. It was my uncle's. He left it—and I think the phrasing went—'To be held in perpetuity, untouched, for the children of the village of Mortimerford, New Hampshire, and to all those who love the beauty of nature.'"

Perdy was touched. "Why, that's very nice."

"The rest of the family didn't think so." He laughed that short, derisive laugh of his and jammed his hands more deeply into his pockets. His wide shoulders were hunched against the increasing cold.

"They thought he was crazy. This land would have been lucrative for housing development, especially this close to Manchester. They tried to break the will. They couldn't, of course. Especially with Algie doing the legal work."

She glanced up at him, studying his stern, dark features. "You don't like your family much, do you?" She couldn't imagine not loving one's family.

"I like them all right," he muttered. "And I'm fond of my youngest sister. She's addlepated, but sweet—even if she loves to meddle. I call her the Preppie Peril. As far as the rest are concerned, I'm just the family maverick, like Uncle Ben." He nodded toward the mountain where his uncle had lived.

He corrected himself. "I should say I was the maverick. My values were always different from theirs. I never gave a damn about the things they held dearest, such as being a pillar of high society. But now I am the very prop and foundation of their genteel fortunes. My mother used to swear the hospital must have given her the wrong son. My brother used to try to tell me I was adopted. I knew I wasn't, so I'd just punch him and say, 'Good! Who wants to be related to you?'"

"Ah—sibling rivalry." She smiled.

"'Rivalry' is too mild a term," he said without smiling. "Good God, what a pair we were. But one doesn't speak ill of the dead, does one?" Suddenly his face looked harder than ever, the line of his mouth like a black scar. He continued walking and said nothing at all, as if all his thoughts had gone elsewhere, deep within.

The dead? she thought. He'd mentioned sisters. Was his brother dead? Was that why he sounded so bitter?

Ben's silence seemed colder than the wind. Oblivious to it, Bummer went galumphing ahead of them, sniffing the snow for the scent of squirrels, snuffling in the brush piles for rabbits.

The edge of the wind grew keener, swifter. They had reached a bend in the path, and though neither said a word, both stopped.

He looked down at her, as if he had suddenly remembered she was there and her presence surprised him. She looked up at him, his sharp-featured face framed by the thrown-back hood of his parka. The wind rippled his dark hair across his forehead.

"What about you?" he asked. "Your family. Where are they?"

She turned her head, hoping he would think her sudden film of tears was caused by the cold, rising wind. "They're gone," she said simply.

"And you miss them." It was a statement, not a question.

She continued to stare off into the distance, through the dark, naked trees. She nodded.

He put his forefinger under her chin and turned her face back toward his. In that instant, she felt something pass between them, knew that again something had subtly changed between them. She was certain of it. Her heart felt as if it had momentarily stopped beating, then had to race to catch up.

They stood that way, ignoring the cold, his black eyes searching her brown ones.

"How different we are, Perdy," he said at last. But whether he was praising or condemning that difference, she could not tell. She could only keep staring up at him.

Something's happening, she thought in bewilderment. *Something I don't understand. What?*

At last he said, "We'd better turn back. It's getting rather intense." His gaze left hers, studied the tossing dark pines, the slender trunks of the pines swaying drunkenly in the rising gale.

She nodded, knowing he wasn't only referring to the weather.

They walked back in a silence that was awkward but companionable. Bummer caught up to them, kicking up a flurry of snow, then cantered ahead, his black coat stark against the world's winter white.

THE LONG AFTERNOON took on a surreal atmosphere of domesticity. Perdy sat cross-legged in the gold chair, crocheting little white angels and red bells. Ben was stretched out before the small fire, his head resting on his parka, reading a book of essays.

Twice he rose, stretched, then sat at the piano, playing moody classical music she couldn't identify.

Surreptitiously she watched his strong hands move across the keys. He had the hands of a musician, all right, or of a surgeon—sure, powerful, sensitive.

He played from memory, which both impressed and oddly depressed her. It demonstrated again his breeding, his culture, his education—all the things she lacked. She remembered what he had said: how different they were.

She shook her head as if to try to clear it. She should be worrying about the gore area, about her furniture, about her shop, and a thousand other prickly details.

Instead, her unruly mind kept drawing back to Ben. Why, if he had wanted to be a doctor, was he running Toynbee's? Why had his face darkened, gone so cold at the memory of his brother? He had implied his brother was dead. Did that have something to do with the complexity and mysteriousness of Ben Squires? His physical presence still occupied her consciousness too—his height, the ebony blackness of his hair and eyes, the masculine angles of his face. Waves of shyness would go scampering through her, and waves of inexplicable restlessness.

The wind rose higher and screamed, ghostlike, through the eaves. But Perdy sat, her crochet hook working, feeling a peculiar, if uneasy, sense of contentment, just having him near.

She went on feeling that way until nine o'clock that evening. It was Perdy's night off from the lounge, and she felt wrapped in her unwarranted sense of well-being, almost secure. She was crocheting a long, twisting garland of yarn, when an ominous rumble came from the basement.

It sounded like a giant that gargled, then choked. There was a gasp and a gagging sound, followed by a mechanical, grating shriek. A shudder went through the house, then everything went still, except for the wind in the eaves and the quiet snapping of the fire.

Perdy's hand flew to her throat, her eyes grew round. "What was that?"

Ben, on the floor, raised his head from his book, frowning. "It sounded like the furnace."

"What did it do? Give birth?"

"I don't know," he said grimly. He rose from the floor in one catlike movement and headed for the stairs, his face full of irate foreboding. Perdy followed him, alarmed, her false sense of peace shattered.

In the utility room Ben leaned over the large square metal bulk. He examined a switch. He frowned. He looked at an oil gauge. He frowned. He slapped the side of a pipe hard, with the flat of his lean hand. A fine shower of soot rained down. He swore.

"What is it?" Perdy asked. She wondered if the mysterious thing were about to explode.

"Your furnace," he said, teeth clenched, "hasn't given birth. Quite the opposite. It's died. It's out."

"Out?" she wailed. All her suppressed nervousness rushed to the surface.

She looked at him in righteous expectation. Why was he looking so perturbed? Why wasn't he doing something about the furnace? Frankie and Nels had always repaired everything that was broken. They were whizzes at such things. "Well, fix it, can't you? You're a man."

"Thanks for the belated acknowledgment," he said dryly. "If you broke your arm, I could fix it. If you wanted a tip on the stock market, I could give it to you. Your furnace is another matter. You'll have to call somebody."

His words seemed to fall on her head like a series of bricks. "A furnace man?" she asked in dismay. "At this time of night? On a *Sunday*?" She had a vision of more of her dollars swirling down a bottomless drain.

She remembered, suddenly, what she had managed to forget all day. She had troubles by the boxcarload, and this man was responsible for all of them. She'd been foolish to feel any warmth toward him.

She turned on her heel to go upstairs and phone the furnace man. "How can a person graduate from Yale and not even know how to fix a furnace?" she muttered darkly. It was certainly a mystery to her.

He followed her, but all he said was, "You may have a point. I'll take it up with the dean." She didn't like the amusement in his voice.

She sat on the living room floor, flipping through the advertising pages of the telephone book. He leaned against the mantel, watching her.

"Did you have the furnace cleaned and checked before you started using it?"

Cleaned? She wondered how on earth one cleaned a furnace. With a feather duster or a mop or what? She shook her head furiously.

"You're going to have to learn, Perdy," he said, staring down at her and shaking his head, "that with the joys of home ownership, there come, alas, responsibilities. Tsk, tsk, not cleaning your furnace." His dark brows were mocking.

She tried to ignore him.

"No," said the answering service of the first furnace man. He couldn't come. He was bravely waging war to revive the heating system of an entire bowling alley.

"No," said the second furnace man hoarsely. He had that horrible flu that was going around; and did she know anything that would really work on a killer headache?

"Maybe," said the third furnace man, elusively.

"But you've got to come tonight," Perdy begged. "I can already feel how cold it's getting."

"Lady, I got other people before you," he said majestically. "Stand in line with everybody else. I'll be there when you see me. Maybe tomorrow, maybe the next day—if you're lucky. You don't like it, call somebody else."

Perdy promised to wait patiently, cheerfully, even gratefully. Then she hung up the phone and shook her fist at it. "Yankees! Furnaces! I never met such rude people—I wish I was in Cloverdale."

Ben, still lounging against the mantel, hands in his pockets, gave her a dark look and one of his rare smiles. "We're not rude, Perdy. Just frank and forthright. There are furnaces in Cloverdale, too. And they break, just like everywhere else."

She wasn't amused. She leaned against the corner, stuck her legs straight out and folded her arms. All her problems came flooding back to her in a troublesome tide.

"You can have the whole frank, forthright lot of them," she answered stonily. "If I was in Cloverdale, this would be your problem."

He sat down, leaning his back against the wall. "No, it wouldn't," he said calmly. "I'd still be the tenant at this point, and you'd be the owner. You'd be responsible for repairs. Even if the roof blew off. Even if all the walls fell down."

"That's not fair," she objected, not liking his patronizing tone nor the mocking light in his black eyes. "If the furnace went out while you were in the house, it should be your problem."

"Perdy, Perdy." He shook his dark head. He drew up his knees and propped his sweatered elbows on them, linking his long fingers together.

He looked half amused, half disgusted. "You don't understand half of what you signed, do you? The seller is always responsible for repairs. Sometimes even after the sale. It depends on the contract."

She didn't answer him. The breakdown of the furnace seemed like the last and possibly fatal blow in a series of disasters designed to destroy not merely her patience, but her spirit. Ben was staring at her with such dark fixity she was beginning to feel a surge of her old enmity toward him.

"Perdy," he said at last. "Just what kind of situation are you getting yourself into in Indiana? What kind of business? How thoroughly have you checked it out?"

"I'm buying a fabric shop," she said defensively. "Don't worry. I know what I'm doing."

She wondered if she really did know what she was doing, and that only worsened her mood. She certainly wasn't going to tell Ben she'd only been in Cloverdale once in her life—or that she'd never even seen the shop.

"Have you checked out the structure of the place? Thoroughly, I mean? Did you have somebody knowledgeable look at everything—the wiring, the plumbing? Did you take good stock of the inventory? Did you go over the books? You can keep accounts, can't you?''

She set her mouth stubbornly. Of course she hadn't done any of those things. Of course she'd never kept accounts, except for the household ones with Nels, and they'd seldom had two spare dimes to rub together. All she'd known was that she'd always had an instinctive understanding of fabrics and what could be done with them. About actual business, she knew next to nothing. Under Ben's questioning, she felt like a person who had wandered into a bad and foolish dream.

He gave a laugh, short and sharp. "Not talking, are you? Oh, come now. Broken furnaces, faulty pipes, even gore areas are all part of owning property. Try maintaining a structure as huge as Toynbee's sometime. You have to learn to expect these things.''

"I'll do just fine in Cloverdale," she insisted. But in spite of the force she put behind the words, it was more of an incantation, a prayer to the gods, than a statement of true conviction.

He rested his chin on his fist and studied her. "When I took over Toynbee's, it was like walking into hell incarnate, Perdy. Ten million troublesome details, all screaming to be solved at once. I wasn't exactly trained for it—but at least I'd been brought up with it. Are you positive you know what you're getting into?''

The more questions he asked, the more childish and heedless she felt. She stiffened. "I told you I know what I'm doing," she said uneasily. But her voice lacked conviction. She wished he would stop watching her like a hawk. She drew up her knees and encircled them with her arms. Cold was seeping into the house fast. The chill nibbled into her flesh, into her bones.

Cloverdale, she thought. Things would be fine if she could just get to Cloverdale. Of course they would. She could not doubt it for one moment.

He watched her as she shivered involuntarily. "Do you want my parka? It'd keep you warmer than anything else. Well, almost anything else..."

She gave him a glance that told him she knew perfectly well what "anything else" meant, and that she wasn't interested. But the look on his face was one of concern, and it confused her. She hugged herself to keep warm.

He rose, went to the closet, and got out his parka. He handed it to her and she took it, draping it around her shaking shoulders. He sat down again, leaning against the wall.

"Why Cloverdale, Indiana, anyway?" he asked. His voice was soft. "What's the charm? You don't look like a small-town girl. What's in Cloverdale besides this shop?"

She didn't want to answer that. She would sound foolish.

"Perdy? I'm talking to you." His voice was low, but edged now with impatience.

The wind shrilled in the eaves, hooting and shrieking, as if to mock her plight. Sleet chattered against the window in myriads of tiny pellets.

"Oh, never mind about Cloverdale," she said miserably. He had no right to ask. And besides, he would never understand how the dream of Cloverdale had sustained her through the loss of Nels and Esmeralda.

He rose and threw another scrap of wood on the small fire. She shivered again and tried to draw his jacket more tightly around her.

"It's not going to work," he said.

His words chilled her. She looked up at him. A small, irrational fear pranced through her.

He ran his fingers through his dark hair. "This fire isn't going to help. The wood's green pine. It doesn't burn well. And I only have a little stacked on the deck. I could go out and gather more, but it'd be wet. Damned sleet."

"Why don't you just burn some money?" Perdy said irritably. "You're rich enough. You've got enough money to practically hound me into the grave with your lawyer. Why not just throw a few thousand on the fire?"

He laughed and turned to face her, his hands in his pockets. "Most women adore me because of my money. You're the first one who's ever held it against me. And I'm not trying to hound you into your grave. The gore area's a messy situation. It needs to be cleared up. That, my dear, is merely good business, as I told you."

"Sam says the gore area never caused any problems before," she countered, defending herself. "Nobody else ever jumped up and down and made a big fuss about it."

He flicked her a cold glance. "That's because this is a tiny village where everyone trusts everyone else. The world at large, I fear, is crueler. And much, much pickier about legal details."

She sighed and could see her breath. "And I really am responsible for getting the furnace fixed?" she asked in resignation. "Are you sure?"

He sighed himself, a sound of sorely tried patience. "It's all in the contract you signed, dammit—it's business again. I'm really beginning to think you don't understand that at all. Not one iota of it."

If he mentioned her ignorance of business one more time, she thought, she would scream. "What I understand," she said, her brown eyes snapping, "is we're going to freeze in here. Just what do you suggest we do?"

He shrugged his wide shoulders. "I don't know. Maybe I'll just stand here awhile, watching you turn bluer. You look incredibly cold. You must have very thin blood. You should take iron pills."

"My blood's as thick as anybody's," she replied, but shivered again. "Stop joking. What are we going to do?"

"Simple." One black brow slanted with amusement. "We go to bed. It's after ten o'clock. There's nothing else we can do. So why don't you hop into your jammies and we'll go beddy-bye.''

Her eyes widened in anger and disbelief. "We? What do you mean *we*? You promised me not to—"

He raised a hand in pacification. "I promised you I wouldn't make any advances—unless expressly invited. I will behave like the gentleman I was raised to be. The most conservative elements of Boston would applaud my self-control. We don't have much choice. We each have something the other wants. You have a bed. But I have something you'll desire even more. Curious?"

"No," Perdy asserted, certain he was trying to be suggestive.

"The item I have is one you will long for, positively lust for, something you will grow, very quickly, to love. It will give you untold satisfaction. It is an electric blanket."

She hugged herself tighter, then went very still, thinking. "Where'd you get an electric blanket?" she asked suspiciously.

"I told you. I went shopping in the village this morning."

An electric blanket, she thought, then shuddered with cold. An electric blanket. She exhaled very carefully, and once more saw her breath.

"I'll even wear my sweatpants," he promised. "I won't lay a hand on you. I'll be a perfect gentleman. Although I'm much more entertaining when I'm not."

"If you're such a gentleman," she countered, "why don't you just let me have the blanket; you could go to a motel."

"Neither of us can go to a motel," he answered easily. "It's Christmastime. And this is a ski area. Every motel between here and Vermont is full. If you're sensible, we can share the blanket—and a little body heat. So why don't we go to bed and get warm—before you start shaking any harder?"

She regarded him warily. He seemed sincere enough, and she was getting so cold she was trembling all over. "Promise—" she began.

"I promised already," he said edgily. "My God, woman, you've already struck me three nearly mortal blows: my arm, my stomach, my foot. I'm not a masochist. Now get ready for bed. I'll warm up the blanket."

This is insane, she thought as she washed her face at the bathroom sink. Her feet danced on the cold floor. Her body was doing some sort of polka to ward off the cold. She took out her contacts and slipped into her warmest nightgown.

It was also her most modest nightgown. In fact, it was positively Victorian, with a high neck, full sleeves and a long, billowing skirt. She put on her glasses and made her way toward the bedroom.

Light fell through the half-opened door. Was she really doing this? She danced about a bit more, wondering if she should flee into the night, brave the sleet, and pound on Sam and Emma Puckett's door, barefoot, an orphan of the storm.

"Are you coming to bed or not?" his gruff voice demanded.

"Turn out the light first." Her voice quavered.

"Oh, hell, Perdy, I've seen women in nightgowns before. And women without nightgowns. Come on. I told you I'd behave, dammit!"

"Turn out the light," she ordered. "Nobody sees me without my makeup!" Or in my glasses, she thought, pulling them off.

She heard him swear, fumble out of bed, and turn out the light. She crept into the darkened room, groped for the bed, and found the covers turned back.

Am I really doing this? she asked herself again. But then her hand touched the warmth of the electric blanket and the heat felt like heaven itself. She slipped, shivering, into the bed, pulling the blankets more tightly around her, burrowing into them like an animal seeking shelter.

"Perdy! You're taking all the blankets!" Ben's voice was disturbingly close to her ear. "You're wrapping yourself up as if you were an enchilada or something."

Her heart pounded and she stiffened. She tried to lie still and let the heat steal through her trembling limbs. The length of his body felt electrifyingly near and she realized, with foreboding, that the bed sagged in the middle.

They were going to be rolling into its valley and colliding together all night. The thought did nothing to quell the tickling in the pit of her stomach, the fluttering sensations throughout her body.

She struggled for a comfortable position as far from him as possible. He groaned and tried to do the same. In a moment, however, they were both sliding toward the bed's sagging center. Each tried to turn over, but soon they were tangled together again, face to face, in the middle of the mattress.

She could feel the hair of his chest tickling her chin. Somehow, her long skirt was askew, and he was lying on it, and his knee was wedged, hard, between her knees.

"You move your leg right now!" she whispered in horror, uncomfortable at the sensations his touch sent tingling up and down her thighs.

"I can't help it if we're both all legs," he muttered, putting his hand on her arm in an attempt to extricate himself. "Hold still, or we're going to be trussed up like mummies."

He moved his leg, but it only went higher, between her thighs. He tugged at the material of her gown, trying to free them both, and his hands sent strange tremors through her body. He tugged again, which only brought her closer to him, her breasts now pressed against his bare chest.

"Oh!" she said, half panicked. She was beginning to have some very bizarre sensations.

"Sorry," he breathed. "Ah! There. I think I've got it." She felt his hands on her hips, his thigh withdrawing from between hers. Her legs suddenly felt cold and unprotected.

"Look," she gasped, trying to inch up the incline of the bed. "This isn't going to work. Ouch!"

He had tried to turn, but his broad shoulder had once again pinned the loose fabric of her gown, this time at the back, pulling it tight against her sensitive breasts.

"Yes it can," he disagreed. "I have lots of experience, and I know it can be done. Hold still."

Then he leaned on his elbow, rearranging the blanket. Her breasts were freed again, but seemed swollen, yearning. "Now listen to me," he breathed in her ear. "We'll try the spoons."

She blinked in disbelief, her senses reeling. "Spoons? What's silverware got to do with this?"

He was silent a moment, leaning above her. She could feel the heat from his body.

"My, my," he whispered. "Another gap in your knowledge. And what an interesting one."

Oh, why, she thought, could he make his voice go like velvet the way he did? Why did she have such a strong urge to turn, and face him, to stop struggling so hard against touching and being touched?

"The spoons, m'dear, is the name of a sleeping position. We're both going to end up in the middle of this bed, whether we like it or not. So stay with your back to me. Now let me fit my body against yours, as if we're a pair of spoons nesting in a drawer."

She felt him settling his body against hers. His chest fitted against her back, his loins against her hips, his long legs curving to rest against the lines of her slightly curled ones. They seemed to fit together perfectly.

"Now," he said against her hair. "You'll just have to put up with this part. I put my arm around you. Like this."

The warmth of his bare arm arched gently over her body, settled around her, drawing her nearer to him. His lean hand rested lightly on her waist.

"There. Now try to lie still. And sleep." He was so close she could feel his breath in her hair. She was so taut that she had never felt less like sleeping in her life.

"Shh. Relax. You're tense as a coiled spring. This is much harder on me than it is on you, I assure you. But I'll keep my promise. Good night now."

"Good night," she managed at last, her voice barely audible. Her heart was beating wildly.

But he was true to his word. In a few moments she felt his muscles grow heavier, somnolent. She felt the regular rise and fall of his broad chest against her back.

She should have felt relieved; instead she was strangely disappointed. She really must be easy to resist. But this was what she had demanded—that he leave her alone. This was what she had wanted.

It was a long time before she could let her muscles ease, snuggle more closely against him and drift toward sleep.

Before she did so, she put her hand on the lean one settled so lightly on her waist. Obeying some odd impulse, she pressed it more firmly against her, feeling the sculpture of its fine, strong bones. He sighed, and laced his fingers through her own. Locked within the safety of his arm, she slept and dreamed she was sixteen again, passing through Cloverdale...

Only the town was not the same. It looked like any other Midwestern town. It looked like a thousand other towns. There was nothing special about it. It was not home. She looked around wildly for Nels, for Frankie and Esmeralda. They were not there. She felt suddenly abandoned, lost, betrayed. She stirred uneasily in her sleep, whimpered. A strong arm tightened around her. A warm mouth brushed the back of her neck.

"Shh. You're fine. I'm here," he murmured.

She sighed and floated back to sleep against the strength of his warm body. She sank back into her dreams. In their velvet mists she thought: *I am home. I'm finally home.*

She awoke only once more during the night, when he mumbled something in his sleep. She blinked awake, then drowsily let her eyes fall shut. Had he spoken to her? Then the word came from him again, in a low, sleepy, unhappy voice. He said a woman's name.

But it was not hers.

CHAPTER SIX

PERDY FINISHED blending her eye shadow, then hugged herself for warmth, staring into the mirror. She studied herself for signs of dissipation, moral decay.

Her reflection stared back, skin very white, eyes very dark, mouth very troubled.

First you lived with the man, her reflection seemed to accuse. Now you have slept in the same bed with him. What's more—you liked it! Shame! You used to be a nice girl, no matter what people thought.

"I haven't done anything wrong," she muttered back to her reflection, unconvinced. She sat down on the edge of the tub to pull on her mukluks. Besides, she wondered, what was he going to think? How would he act? What do you say to a man after you've spent the night in his arms? She had no idea.

What was she going to do about her own feelings? She remembered his ragged utterance of another woman's name. What had it been? Sharon? Sheila? Shirley? She was disturbed. She may have been the woman in his arms, but she hadn't been the woman on his mind.

She stood up and buckled a wide black belt around the waist of her warmest sweater, a hip-length gold one with full sleeves and tight wrists. She had on black wool slacks cut like a Russian cossack's. She looked like a woman of the world, even if she wasn't. She remembered Esmeralda's motto: "When in doubt: brazen it out."

Her teeth chattering, she put on an old knee-length cape of brown rabbit fur. She'd made it, years ago, from a coat she'd bought in a thrift shop. The fur had seen better days but the cape would keep her warmer than anything else. She went to brazen it out.

Just as she began descending the stairs she heard the phone ring. Ben answered it. Maybe it was Sam, she hoped, finally getting her out of this mess. But when she heard Ben talking, she paused, her hand on the banister.

"Look, darling, I told Algie not to give anybody this number. I know he can't withstand your considerable charms, but I don't want to be called."

Perdy's back stiffened. Who was he calling "darling," and who had such considerable charm?

"Cheryl," he sighed, "I'm fine. Of course I'm alone. I said I'm fine. I just need to be by myself."

Cheryl, she thought. Had that been the name he'd uttered in his sleep? And he was lying; he was far from alone. He'd just spent the night in her bed. Her hand rested, frozen, on the banister.

"Cheryl," he growled, "do anything you want about the wedding. I told you, spare no expense. Put everything on my tab. Of course, I'm not going to walk out on you at the last minute. I'll be there. Cheryl—I told you—I just need to be by myself for a while."

Wedding? Perdy thought, her stomach churning as if she were going to be sick. He was getting married? Was that why he was off by himself in New Hampshire—some sort of last-minute retreat before his marriage? Was he treating her as some sort of last-minute fling?

"Yes, Cheryl," he said, a note of weariness in his voice. "I think you'll look lovely in ivory silk. No, I don't think orchids would be too flashy. Yes, I think the Mediterranean would be splendid for a honeymoon. Yes, dammit, I'm fine. But don't call me here again, all right? Fine, darling. Yes, yes, yes, I know. I love you, too."

A wedding and orchids and a honeymoon in the Mediterranean, she thought, feeling another sickening wave of anger. And he had said, "I love you." Getting married certainly hadn't kept him from making advances, the two-timer! She felt almost sorry for Cheryl, who seemed to be begging for his reassurance.

She heard him say goodbye, hang up the phone and go into the kitchen. She continued down the stairs and went into the kitchen to make her coffee. She felt disillusioned and angry enough to kick him clear to Vermont, then disgusted that she should even care. Cheryl should be the one who was hurt and angry. What kind of man went off and left the woman he loved at Christmas, while he cavalierly tried to seduce the first girl who crossed his path?

Ben stood at the counter, eating scrambled eggs and sprouts off a paper plate. He wore his shearling coat over a heavy red ski sweater. His black eyes looked her over with proprietary interest.

"Good morning, Perdy," he said easily. "You're looking very Siberian this morning. Have a good night?"

"I've had better," she replied coldly. "Much better." As she filled the pot with water she could feel his gaze following her movements.

"You know," he offered, "I was lying in bed this morning, watching you sleep. You looked so innocent. Like a little girl with tousled dark hair. Not a bit like some Russian warrior-princess from the wild steppes. Know what? I don't think you've had 'better nights' at all—have you?"

She stood before the stove, her arms crossed beneath the cape. She felt her body go still as if it had actually frozen. He had guessed her inexperience and was mocking it.

"My nights are no concern of yours," she said stiffly. Her fingers gripped her upper arms more tightly. "And you have a lot of nerve. I overheard your conversation on the phone. You were right. You're not a very nice man at all."

He lifted one wide shoulder in a shrug. "You've got quite a bit of nerve yourself—eavesdropping. And what about you? Against all appearances, are you a nice girl?"

She was intensely conscious of his gaze burning into her back. More strongly than ever she sensed his sexual magnetism, and she cursed that awareness.

"You're either not what you seem, Perdy," he muttered at last, his voice cold and speculative. "Either that—or the most accomplished tease I've ever met. Whichever, you're playing with dynamite."

His words struck like a blow. He was calling her a tease? She might put on a bold front to hide a thousand insecurities, but she would never promise to marry one man and flirt with another. She valued loyalty above all else.

She turned to face him, her upper lip rising in disdain. "And maybe you're playing with dynamite yourself," she said, her voice dangerously soft, almost purring. "I can put on quite a fireworks display myself. So be careful."

She turned her back to him again and got out the instant coffee.

"That," he snarled, banging the counter with the flat of his hand, "is exactly what I mean. How am I supposed to take that? As a warning or an invitation?"

"As a statement of fact," she replied, tired of playing his games. "You figure it out. You went to Yale."

"Do you know what I ought to do to you?" he asked, his gravelly voice taut.

The sudden menace emanating from him both frightened and excited her, but her anger was stronger than either emotion. "Yes." She bit off the word. "Leave me alone, like you promised. I have better things to do than be part of your flock of Juliets while you play Romeo. Bye-bye. Boola-boola, and all that."

Suddenly she felt him turn his anger off, cast it away as if she weren't worthy of it. He was shutting her out, quickly, cleanly, coldly. "Say anything you like," he answered, his voice devoid of concern. "But never scorn the sacred cheer of Yale. Always say boola-boola with great reverence—if that's an emotion you're capable of."

She turned to face him. "Boola, boola," she said again, with no reverence at all.

"Of all the women in the great, wide world," he said, dark eyes dangerous, "it had to be you here, didn't it? It had to be you."

THEY SPENT MOST of the day in silence, Perdy furiously crocheting as she shivered in her chair, Ben lying before the fire, reading. He ignored her with a thoroughness she could only marvel at. She might have been a mote of dust.

Yesterday's illusion of companionship was gone. Perversely, she missed it, but knew she was far safer without it, especially after learning about Cheryl and her considerable charms and the wedding with orchids.

She planned her afternoon carefully. At three o'clock she'd take a walk, just to get away from him. She'd bring a small Christmas tree back from the woods and set it up. If he didn't like it, that would be just too bad.

At four, she'd leave for work early, stop in the village and buy her own electric blanket. She couldn't afford it, but she wasn't spending another night beside him—beside somebody else's fiancé. He could go right back to sleeping on the floor, like the beast he was.

When she rose, he glowered up at her from his place beside the fire.

"Where do you think you're going?"

"For a walk," she said sharply, heading for the hall closet. She changed her cape for her jacket and cap. "Any objections? I'm going to get my Christmas tree," she said, pulling on a glove.

He rose, supporting himself on his elbow, the straight line of his brows severe. "Yes, I have objections. It sleeted half the night, then snowed on top of it. Under that snow, it's slick as glass. You could fall and break one of those long racehorse legs. And how do you propose to cut down a tree? With your sharp little tongue?"

"There's an old axe behind the water heater downstairs. I'll save my sharp little tongue for cutting you down."

"I used to wish I'd find a woman with enough spirit to stand up to me. I should have had my head examined. If you go out, you'll probably break a leg and be crushed by a tree. The wind's up again. Those birches can snap off like toothpicks. One could come down right on top of you."

"I quake," she said sarcastically. "I quail. I quiver with terror. Does it daunt me? No. I'm going out. Stay by your fire, Felix Faintheart."

He shot her a dark look of disgust, rolled onto his side and opened his book again. "I don't know what's got into you today," he sneered, "but somebody ought to spank it out of you. And I'm becoming sorely tempted. Women!"

If he didn't like women, she thought, tossing her head, maybe he shouldn't collect so many.

Perdy fetched the axe—an old, rusted one with a cracked handle—and marched through the kitchen and out onto the deck. She whistled twice for Bummer, then set off for the path. It was almost invisible under the fresh snow.

Ben had been right, she thought with dismay. The frozen sleet beneath the snow was treacherous. She slipped, slid, and more than once nearly lost her balance. She wished she weren't carrying the axe. The thought of falling on its rusty blade made her feel queasy.

He had been right about the wind, too. It mourned crazily through the pines, a cold, horrible sound. Broken pine limbs, weighted with ice and snapped off by the wind, lay like snags across her path.

She saw two birches down. The others were swaying wildly in the wind, their slender white trunks straining painfully. She heard a sound like a crack of thunder, and her heart leaped in fear, knowing another birch must have crashed to the cold forest floor.

Bummer joined her at last, and she felt a little safer, grateful for his company. He, too, reeled and slid on the hidden ice, his black legs skidding from beneath him.

At last they reached the pond, where the trees were less dense, and she sighed in relief. A scrubby little pine grew near the weathered shack by the old lifeguard tower.

She raised the axe and struck it against the tree's small trunk. The axe was so dull, her swings so tentative and inexpert, it took her a long time to chop through. At last the tree shuddered, fell, and she wrenched it loose from the last strips of bark holding it together.

She turned to whistle for Bummer, then stopped, the tree still in her hand. Bummer was on the far shore of the pond, in hot pursuit of a rabbit, which now, in its desperate attempt to escape, was bounding out across the ice. Without hesitation, the big dog pursued its leaping quarry.

"Bummer!" she screamed. "Bummer!"

But Bummer, sliding and stumbling across the ice, only kept up his awkward gallop, while the rabbit streaked past the center of the pond and toward the other shore.

Suddenly the ice beneath the big dog gave way like a weak membrane, and Bummer was no longer on the surface of the pond. He was struggling in a pit of icy water, a black hole that gaped in the whiteness.

The rabbit skittered to safety, but Bummer was trapped, floundering. Each time he tried to fling his forepaws onto the ice to pull himself free, the ice gave way, pitching him back into the frigid depths.

"Bummer!" she screamed again. She started to run toward him.

"What in h—" She whirled and saw Ben behind her, his black hair whipping in the wind.

"He fell through!" she cried. "He was chasing a rabbit. We've got to save him!" She began to run again in hopes she could reach the thrashing dog.

Ben's arm jerked her back roughly. "If that ice won't hold a dog, it won't hold you," he rumbled, giving her arm a shake. "I knew you'd get yourself in some kind of trouble out here."

"I'm not in trouble," she said, stamping her boot defiantly. "Bummer is! Are we going to stand here and watch him drown?"

"Be quiet," he said shortly, taking the axe from her. "And stand back."

He strode to the front of the weather-beaten shed, raised the axe, and brought it down against the lock of the door. The wood splintered beneath the blow, and he kicked the door open.

Perdy followed him. Bummer was crying now, yelping in terror. Her heart hammered wildly.

Ben kicked aside an old wooden rowboat with rotting boards, and found a long coil of fraying rope, stiff from the cold. A filthy, battered life preserver with a canvas cover hung on a rusty nail. He snatched it down, found a smaller coil of nylon boating rope, and pushed his way back out of the shack.

He stripped off his gloves, jerking the rigid, frozen rope to loosen it. He tied the two ropes together, and lashed the life preserver to the end with the lighter nylon cord.

"What are you doing?" Perdy demanded. "Are you crazy? What good's that going to do?"

He gave her a quick, withering look. "A drowning dog is like a drowning person. He'll try to climb on anything—including this. If I can throw it out far enough. But I'll have to get farther out on the ice. I'll never reach him from here."

"Ben! Don't!"

She watched him make his way out onto the pond's surface, testing each step carefully. The ice near the shore was more solid. Her stomach contracted with fear as she saw him suddenly move backward when the ice where he'd just stepped cracked, fracturing like the surface of a broken mirror.

At least fifty feet still separated him from the dog, but Ben couldn't risk stepping out any farther—he'd have to try from there. Bummer strove once more to pull himself up onto the ice. Once more it gave way beneath him, and he began swimming in crazed circles.

Ben drew back his arm and heaved the preserver toward the widening hole. It fell short. He reeled it back in, shucked off his bulky parka, picked up the preserver, and threw it again. Perdy saw his long body wrench with the effort.

Again the throw fell short. He snatched the heavy preserver back, tried again. And again. And again. Only Bummer's black head was visible now. He had stopped trying to climb out onto the ice. He floundered in the dark water, his mouth open. He was moving more slowly. He was wearing out.

She heard Ben swear. He rubbed his arm and shoulder. He pulled in the life preserver again, and stood, panting a moment, rubbing his right shoulder. Then he picked up the life preserver again, hurling it like an awkward, heavy discus, and even from where she stood, she heard his grunt of pained effort.

The preserver landed within a few feet of the black hole, bounced with a thud, and slid into the water.

"Come on, Bummer!" Perdy called, clenching her fists. "Come on!"

In panic the big dog tried to climb on the float, heaving himself up out of the water. At last he clambered on awkwardly, his front paws hooking over it, and Ben began to pull, inching backward on the ice.

The thinner ice surrounding the dog broke away, and Ben pulled harder, a strong, steady pull that would break the ice without shaking the dog's precarious, scrambling hold.

Perdy held her breath. The ice stopped giving way. "Call him!" Ben ordered sharply. "Call him, Perdy, dammit!"

"Bummer!" she cried out, her voice shaky. "Here, Bummer! Here, boy!" She gave her whistle, although her lips seemed to have turned to ice.

Slowly, wearily, the dog half crawled, half scrabbled over the unsteadily bobbing preserver to the edge of the ice, and hauled himself out. He collapsed heavily, and Perdy feared he would fall through again, but he did not. Then he rose, staggered to his feet, shook himself weakly, and began a drunken stumble toward the shore.

Perdy kept calling. The big dog fell again and again, but always rose, shaking and limping toward her.

When he reached the edge of the shore, Ben scooped him up, wrapping his parka around the soaked black fur. He carried the dog with its head lower than its body and pressed against his chest.

"You're going to catch pneumonia yourself," Perdy said shakily, trailing behind him. "And you're holding him upside down!"

"I'm trying to get blood to his brain," Ben said, over his shoulder. "He's in a slight state of shock. Now get back to the house before something happens to you, too."

She hurried after him, not even aware that she still had the little Christmas tree by the trunk in her hand. Ben's wide shoulders were hunched against the wind and cold as he cradled the heavy dog to his chest.

"FILL THE BATHTUB," Ben ordered when they were back at the house. "And get some blankets." He stretched Bummer on the kitchen floor, his lean hands running expertly over the dog's trembling body. He examined the paws carefully and laid his fingers against Bummer's chest, feeling his heartbeat.

Apparently satisfied, he hoisted the dog up and carried him up to the bathroom, rubbing him briskly with their one limp towel.

He stripped off his soaked sweater and knelt, bare-chested, to test the water in the tub with his elbow, then lowered Bummer into the warmth.

The dog thrashed briefly in terror at the feel of water, but Ben held him fast and firmly, soothing him. "There's milk in the refrigerator," he told Perdy. "Go heat it up—warm, not hot. And put a couple of tablespoons of brandy in it. It's under the counter. And bring me a sweatshirt."

She didn't question his orders. She went downstairs to the kitchen and warmed some milk on the burner, then ran upstairs and snatched a gray sweatshirt from the closet shelf.

"Hold him," he told her. "He's calmed down now." She knelt beside the tub and stroked Bummer's still-quaking body. He whimpered and then hiccoughed.

Ben stood up, pulling the sweatshirt down over his head and his bare, bronzed chest with its thick mat of black hair. Then he knelt beside Perdy, taking charge of the dog again, running more hot water into the tub.

"He smells awful," she said, narrowing her nostrils.

"He smells alive, which is all that matters. Go watch the milk. I've got to work on these paws. Frostbite could cripple him." He began kneading Bummer's feet, one at a time.

Half an hour later, Bummer was standing shakily on the bathroom floor, while Ben dried him with one of Perdy's blankets.

He held the big dog steady. Bummer lapped at the brandylaced milk, shuddered, retched, and quietly threw up.

Perdy winced, but Ben cleaned the mess up expertly. "Got rid of some of the ice water, too, old boy? Here, try again." He held the pan carefully, so Bummer could drink only slowly.

"Now," Ben said, looking at Perdy. "Go down to the basement. I noticed some old footstools down there. Bring them up and throw one on the fire. We've got to keep this old pirate warm." He bowed his dark head over the dog again, and Perdy swallowed hard, watching the lean hands, so strong yet surprisingly gentle, moving over the dog's muscles.

The footstools. Esmeralda's footstools, which she'd been given by the legion, to help her reach cupboards, high shelves, window blinds. Perdy had been going to give them to the Salvation Army. They had reminded her too poignantly of Esmeralda. But she brought two upstairs, and with a pang, put one on the dying fire.

Ben came down to the living room carrying the huge dog, now wrapped in a dry blanket, in his arms. He set him down before the fire.

"Will he be all right?" she asked.

"This old wolverine? Oh, yes. He'll live to mooch another day. He's tough. Get me an aspirin, will you?"

She obeyed, then watched as Ben broke a corner of it off and thrust the rest down Bummer's throat with one quick, sure movement.

The big dog shook his head, flicking out his tongue in distaste. Then he sighed deeply, and lay down. He kicked his big paws ineffectually, then closed his eyes and sighed again.

Perdy stood watching him, her heart aglow with satisfaction. She couldn't help admiring Ben, admiring him with all her heart. The room was almost dark and the firelight danced on his black hair.

Darkness, she thought with alarm, glancing at her watch. It was almost five—she'd be late for work!

"Where are you going?" Ben demanded as she raced up to her room to change her boots and get her black cape.

"I'm late for work!" she wailed. She changed quickly, snatched up her gloves and ran downstairs and out the door, hatless.

Then, shivering, she sat at the wheel of the van, trying to start it. The motor gave a sick chug, a grating cry, and died.

She tried again and again. She swore. She fought back tears. The day had been emotional enough without this.

She tried again, biting her lower lip. She hit the steering wheel with a frustrated thump. She looked out the window and saw Ben standing at the side of the van, opening her door.

"What's wrong now?" he asked, as if his patience, like her own, was at its fraying end.

"The van won't start," she said miserably, crossing her arms over the wheel and burying her face in them.

"Oh, come on," he said gruffly, giving her shoulder a shake. She flinched from his touch. "You're not going to let one more measly disaster get you down, are you? I'll drive you. Don't get dramatic on me."

His hand was on her arm, and she let him draw her out of her seat, fatalistically let him lead her to his car, the onyx-black BMW.

"And how am I supposed to get home?" she asked, settling into the passenger seat.

He slammed the door shut, went around the car and got in. "Logically, I suppose that I'll pick you up," he said, a sardonic quirk to his mouth.

"I don't want to impose," she said uneasily. He was being, in his own brusque way, too nice. She was beginning to like him again—in spite of herself, and in spite of the conversation she had overheard with Cheryl. The feeling was a dangerous one.

"You won't move out of my house, but you hate imposing." He raised his eyebrows as if he found both her statement and herself hard to believe.

"My house," she corrected him. Suddenly she wished Sam had called. Wasn't he ever going to get her out of this maddening situation?

He started the car and they set out in strained silence.

"I'm glad you were there," she admitted to him at last. She supposed she owed him that much. "Thanks for saving

Bummer. What made you come out? Were you looking for wood?''

His black-gloved fingers clenched the steering wheel tighter. "I was looking for you," he muttered. "I heard another birch go down, and I figured with your luck, it had landed right on your head. An intriguing thought, since it might possibly have knocked some sense into it."

Then he grimaced, setting his teeth, and gave an involuntary grunt of pain.

She studied his lean profile. "What's wrong?"

"I strained a muscle, I think," he said. "Trying to rescue that ox." He willed the pain out of his face and gave her a mocking half-smile. "Impressive, wasn't I? If I'd thrown that way at Yale, we might have won more than two games."

"Yale." She smiled in spite of herself. "Where you were, in all modesty, a quarterback?"

"In overwhelming modesty. As befits a true hero."

His eyes held hers for a second before resting on the road again. Perdy felt a little frisson of something go shooting through her, starting the familiar flutter in her midsection. Whatever it was that existed between them was exerting itself again, frightening her. She stared straight ahead and lapsed into silence for the rest of the ride.

He walked her to the door of the lounge, in spite of her protestations. "There," he said, by the side entrance. "Another domestic crisis weathered together. This is getting to be almost like a marriage, Perdy."

Marriage indeed, she thought. It was obviously a word he took lightly.

BEN CAME TO PICK HER UP EARLY, and she could see the disapproval in his eyes as he watched her go from table to table announcing the last call for drinks. She supposed she did look thoroughly disreputable in the little red costume with its sequins and fur trim and the black net stockings. He waited in the entrance as she quickly changed.

"Can't you find a better job than that? A girl with your resources to fall back on?" he challenged as soon as they were in the car. "Don't you see how the men watch those legs of yours? Why on earth are you working there?"

"What resources? I took the first job I could get," she replied defensively. "I've got debts mounting up. Remember me? I'm the one who didn't want to be here. I thought I'd be in Cloverdale by now. So let's change the subject. How's Bummer?"

His look told her he would like to challenge her further, but his mouth was set as stubbornly as hers. "Bummer's resting well. He's just exhausted, that's all. He should be his old, obnoxious self by morning."

Morning, she thought. It reminded her that she and Ben had to spend another night together. With a sinking feeling she remembered she hadn't had time to buy an electric blanket.

He seemed to read her thoughts. "Stiff upper lip, Perdy. I called about my furniture and it'll be here tomorrow. Bummer's got the fireplace staked out as his territory, and you and I can double up again. Don't worry. I'll be pure as the driven snow."

She would too, she vowed. But weariness and frustration welled through her. She tried to think about Cloverdale, but it didn't help. She would probably lose the shop anyway. It almost didn't matter any longer. The only thing that mattered was getting away from Ben. She was tired of fighting her attraction to him. They had nothing in common, they came from different worlds, and he belonged to somebody else—even if he conveniently forgot about it.

They finally reached the house and Bummer raised his head in greeting when they entered the living room, gave a halfhearted "woof" and a thump of his massive tail. Then he stretched out again, snoring.

Ben knelt to check him. Perdy threw her cape over the gold chair, then stood, watching and shivering in the chill air of the house. The furnace still wasn't fixed.

Ben looked up at her. The fire gilded the aristocratic planes of his face. "You look tired, Perdy. And I know I'm tired. Let's have a brandy, then go to bed."

She nodded, then sat cross-legged in front of the fire, staring into it. Another of Esmeralda's little footstools was burning brightly. Suddenly she felt sad and lonely, and confused. Ben rose, went to the kitchen, and returned with two paper cups and a tube of something.

"Cheers," he said, handing her a cup of brandy. "I put up your tree for you." He nodded toward the corner.

The little tree, scrawny and bare, stood there, its trunk wedged between a pair of heavy stones.

"Oh." She was touched. He must have hated doing that. He was such a puzzling man. "You didn't have to," she said, her voice throatier than usual.

"You wanted it so badly," he said gruffly. "I've made your Christmas tough enough already. I'm not very nice to be around this time of year. Which is probably why you haven't been so nice today yourself. I don't blame you."

He sat down at the other side of the fireplace. Bummer stretched, a dark heap, between them. Ben pulled off his sweatshirt, and Perdy felt her heart do a small, Victorian fainting spell at the sight of his broad chest. He began to rub liniment on his shoulder, his arm, his back.

"You know," he said, his dark eyes playful in the dancing light from the flames, "in the short time we've been together, you've practically decimated me. I've sustained more physical damage than the time my polo pony fell on me."

Polo, she thought, watching his handsomely boned hand massage his shoulder. How different their backgrounds were. She had never even seen a polo match. Did Cheryl play polo, as well? she wondered. Or did women play polo? She didn't even know.

But the smell of the liniment was intimate and deeply nostalgic. She remembered Frankie's deft hands working liniment into Nels's huge, punished body.

"Give me some help with my back, will you?" he said, gritting his teeth. "I can't reach the worst spot."

She hesitated. "All right," she said slowly. She had given Nels rubdowns from time to time; she knew how to soothe an aching muscle.

His black eyes met her dark ones, and he handed her the tube across Bummer's sleeping body.

She rose, then knelt behind him, squeezing the lotion onto her palm. Rhythmically she began to work it into the firm, broad muscles of his back and shoulder. She moved her hand slowly, the liniment making her fingers tingle.

Then she began using both hands. She moved them in sensual circles against the firm, smooth skin. It was as if she were becoming hypnotized by the feel of him, could go on touching him forever.

"Perdy," he said, his voice low and rough. "I think you'd better stop." His hand reached out, grasping her wrist. "No more," he said, releasing her abruptly.

"Finish your brandy," he ordered. He slipped the sweatshirt back on.

She returned to her place by the fire, her knees trembling. She sipped the soothing heat of the brandy. It seemed to course through her deeply, mingling with another, brighter fire within her.

Their eyes met. "Don't ever touch me that way again," he said. "Unless you want—unless the terms of our relationship are going to change."

She took another sip of the brandy, feeling her face burning. She said nothing. She hadn't meant to touch him that way. She just had. This time it was her fault that his eyes were searing into hers with such fire, and she knew it.

"What's wrong with you, anyway?" he asked sharply. "Sometimes you act as if you don't have any real idea of what goes on between men and women. As if you don't know what you—''

He didn't finish his sentence. He rose, looming far above her. "I'm going to bed. Will you be coming up soon?"

She shook her head. "No. Not soon. Not for a long time."

She was afraid again, more afraid of her own emotions than of him. It would be so easy for him to make love to her. It would mean nothing to him. Nothing at all. One last, meaningless affair before he married Cheryl. But it wouldn't be meaningless for her—she was beginning to understand that it wouldn't be that way for her at all. She had tried and tried to withstand his attraction and had failed.

He said no more. He turned and left the room.

She sipped her brandy, staring into the dying flames for a long time. The room seemed empty now, the house too silent.

She spun the paper cup between her palms, images of the day going through her mind: she, standing as still as if frozen on the stairs, listening to him talk on the phone; Ben, coatless, on the ice, trying to hurl the preserver toward the struggling dog; Ben, tall, efficient, absolutely in charge, carrying the huge dog wrapped in his parka; Ben kneeling, his fine hands sure and gentle on Bummer's shaking body; Ben, shirtless and golden beside the fire, her hands touching him.

The cold began to creep into her like some painful form of common sense. She imagined what Esmeralda would say: "A man who is about to be married, is a man to put out of your mind. Marriage, kiddo, is sacred."

According to Esmeralda, everything was very simple. You fell in love once, with the man you were to marry, and you saved yourself for him. Those were the rules, and woe unto whosoever broke them.

Perdy knew she couldn't sit in the living room all night. There wasn't enough wood to keep the fire going that long, and without it, she'd freeze. At last she went upstairs and quietly put on her nightgown in the dark, then slipped into bed beside him. He was asleep. She could tell by his breathing.

He stirred, and as she lay, tense and filled with forbidden yearning, he drew her to him, into the same position in which they had slept the night before. His strong arm curled around her, but this time his hand rested not on her waist, but lightly on the curve of her breast.

He stirred again, moaned almost inaudibly. She lay still, feeling her breast swell against the accidental and tantalizing touch of his slim fingers.

She knew that if he so much as breathed her name, it would take all her moral strength not to turn to him, as wrong as it would be.

But the only sounds were the dying December wind outside and his breathing, deep and even, beside her.

"How will I know when I'm in love?" she had often asked Esmeralda.

Esmeralda's pretty face would twist into an impish grin and she would offer the oldest answer in the world: "Don't worry, kiddo. You'll know."

It hadn't made any sense then. Now it did.

She sighed unhappily, snuggled her head against Ben's bare chest, and tried to sleep.

CHAPTER SEVEN

PERDY WAS AWAKENED by a thud, much like that of a falling appliance striking cement, and Bummer began to bark.

Perdy groaned, listening to the racket. Footsteps echoed, voices boomed, and there was the sound of objects being shifted and reshifted. Ben's movers were here.

She reached for her glasses, blinked blearily, wrapped the electric blanket around her shoulders and went to the window, trailing the cord of the blanket like a tail. A red moving van was parked in the drive, and a man was coming up the walk, carrying an antique rocking chair under one arm and an umbrella stand in the other.

Groaning, she slipped into the same clothes she'd worn the day before and fled to the bathroom to put on her makeup. She fluffed up her bangs as best she could, and headed downstairs to the living room where she nearly collided with a burly man carrying an enormous box marked Lamp. He swore at her.

"Watch it, lady," he growled, sidestepping her and giving her a nasty look.

"You watch it," she snapped back. "Or I'll stuff you into a box. And it won't be marked Lamp. It'll be marked Dead Man."

"Huh!" he snorted. "You got some Christmas spirit."

She ignored him. Why should she have any Christmas spirit, she wondered, when her life was in shambles and she was marooned with Boston's answer to Don Juan?

Ben appeared from the kitchen. He had a cup of coffee in his hand, which he made her take.

"Drink this," he ordered, his mouth twisting at the edge. "Remember, I know what you're like before you've had your coffee. That's the wonderful thing about living with a woman. You get to know her so well. This place is chaotic enough without you murdering the moving men."

He steered her into the kitchen. "Look," he said with an expansive gesture. "Behold the luxury—a table—even chairs. Even—" his slim hand indicated a coffee machine on the counter "—real coffee. Now drink the eight cups it takes to make you human."

She sat down self-consciously at the antique pine table. He was certainly a bundle of cheer, she thought, treating her as lightly as if they had slept on separate continents. She remembered his upcoming wedding and suddenly disliked him very, very much.

He was bent over a carton, stripping away layers of packing paper. The kitchen was stacked haphazardly with boxes.

He finally pulled out and examined a horrible-looking black cast-iron kangaroo. He surveyed it with satisfaction. "Ahh. No harm done. One of the movers dropped the box earlier."

She studied the creature in disbelief. "What is that thing? It woke me up, you know."

The kangaroo was a foot high and had a particularly vacuous expression on its iron face.

"My kangaroo. My Uncle Ben left it to me. He brought it back from Australia. It's rumored he stole it from the finest house of ill repute in Brisbane. I always loved it with a passion."

"Loved it?" Perdy asked, shaking her head. She took another sip of coffee. "How could you possibly even like it?"

He tossed her a black, mocking look. "I like her because she's an exemplary lady. She stays where she should—in my bedroom. And she never talks back. Unlike some people I could name."

"Does Cheryl know your idea of an exemplary lady?" she asked sarcastically.

"Yes. And it appalls her. But what can she do about it? She has to take me the way I am or not at all."

His tone implied he didn't mind Cheryl's feelings in the least. He seemed altogether too pleased with himself this morning. He hoisted the kangaroo easily and carried it upstairs to the bedroom, whistling.

Perdy drank two more cups of coffee and ate a stale cracker spread with even staler peanut butter. She'd been eating nothing but crackers and peanut butter since noon the day before. She was feeling edgy. She watched, gloomily, as one of the moving men unpacked the kitchen cartons and began loading the cupboards with china and glassware.

She threaded her way between moving men and cartons to the living room. The phone now sat on an antique pine end table, next to an oversize brown velvet couch. She dialed the garage and told them her van wouldn't start.

The man on the other end told her they would send a tow truck in case the van had to be taken in, and that she would have to pay cash. Cash, she thought forlornly, setting down the receiver. She should start looking for a second job. She was beginning to feel like the little match girl of the fairy tale who froze to death on Christmas Eve.

She was further depressed by the sight of Ben's furniture. It made Esmeralda's house seem somehow foreign, transformed. The living room now looked rich and masculine, forcing away any memory of Esmeralda's presence.

The furniture, with the exception of the couch and an expensive stereo system, was antique. Her gold chair remained, looking like a poor relative at a gathering of rich ones.

Her unhappy reveries were interrupted by the arrival of the furnace man. He descended into the basement, where his rattles, rumbles, crashes, and banging lasted for about an hour.

Then, emerging from the basement, sooty but imperious, he handed her a bill that made her heart stop beating. She swallowed hard, but scribbled a check, her fingers rebelling at the amount she was forced to fill in.

Ben came down from the bedroom and threw himself full-length on the couch, putting his hands behind his head. He watched her as she added up the balance in her checking account, frowned at the small number, then refigured it.

"I see we have heat again," he said cheerfully. "Happy?"

His careless grace on the long couch and the insouciant arrogance of his dark face offended her. He looked far too smug and in command of things.

"I'm ecstatic," she retorted. "Poverty always makes me ecstatic."

"Tsk, tsk," he said, shaking his head ruefully. "As a poet from around these parts once warned pretty young things, 'Provide, provide.' Maybe you should sell your jewelry if you're really so poor. But I imagine you'll survive."

No thanks to you, she thought. What did he mean, sell her jewelry? It was probably worth a dollar and ninety-eight cents. The door bell rang, and she went to answer it. This time it was a thin boy who had arrived from the garage with a tow truck.

She grabbed her jacket from the closet and went out to the van with him. She stood beside him, hopping with cold, as he peered into the mysterious innards of the engine.

He muttered sinister things about solenoids and flywheels with broken teeth.

"How much?" she asked, realizing it was the question she asked most often these days.

He adjusted his greasy cap. "Well, we're probably talkin' a couple hundred all told. Too bad."

She paid him the tow fee, and with a sinking heart watched him pull away the van, which hung suspended from a chain like a small dead whale.

The moving men were clearing the empty cartons out of the house, piling them at the edge of the drive for the trash pickup. Perdy shoved her hands into her pockets and, head down, walked back into the house. She would most certainly have to get another job if the deal didn't close soon. She had to call Sam Puckett.

The moving men were leaving, and Ben was on the phone, his lean face dark with restrained anger. "I mean it, Cheryl. Please stop calling. No, dammit, your place isn't with me. I don't give a damn about Christmas. I just want to be by myself—can't you understand that? If you come up here, I'll choke the life out of you, and then how are you going to walk down the aisle? Fine. Fine. Fine. I am not living with 'some woman.' Algie talks too much. Goodbye."

He set the receiver down irritably. Perdy looked at him, appalled. "How can you treat that poor girl like that? She obviously loves you and you talk to her horribly," she said, bridling at his rudeness.

"She's hardly a 'poor girl' and she knows better than to bother me. And love is not an emotion that terribly impresses me," he snapped.

"You ought to tell her the truth," Perdy challenged. "It sounds as if she knows I'm here. It's all perfectly innocent. You're making her Christmas miserable."

"You're none of her business," he said. He cocked an eyebrow. "And come to think of it, she's none of yours. Stop eavesdropping, and stop harping about her. Christmas—is there no end to it?"

He stalked upstairs to the empty guest room that he would no doubt make his own. She heard him hammering: hanging pictures, no doubt, and ruining Esmeralda's plaster. What was his real problem with Christmas anyway? she wondered angrily. It had to be more than his experiences at

Toynbee's—something deeper, but what, she didn't know. How could he be so cruel to Cheryl if he loved her?

She shed her jacket, then flopped dispiritedly into the gold chair, eyeing Ben's furniture. The living room really did seem to be his now. It had a strong, old-family moneyed look. Bummer lay on a Persian carpet before the fire, as if he had been accustomed all his life to dozing on priceless rugs.

Ben might have money, she thought grumpily, but he didn't have many morals, and he was lacking in plain civility as well. She tried not to think of him and to concentrate on counting the financial leeches sucking the lifeblood out of her bank account.

She had paid the moving company for delivering her furniture to Cloverdale, where it was now in storage—expensive storage—indefinitely.

The house payment was due, the taxes were due, the utility bills were due. The furnace bill had practically knocked her to her knees, and the repairs for the ailing van might be the death blow.

As the final coup de grace, she didn't even know if she'd have to have the furniture sent back from Cloverdale, if she would ever get her shop or not. She listened to Ben hammering away in the bedroom. With a guilty rush she remembered last night, the hard warmth of his long body curved to hers, his strongly boned hand brushing her breasts, and how she had wanted, almost yearned to turn toward him. Had she been crazy? He was no good, no good at all.

At least he had his own bed now, but even that didn't seem safety enough. She wanted to get away from him, away from his Prince-of-Darkness attractiveness, his hatred of Christmas, his stormy engagement to the luckless Cheryl.

She picked up the phone and dialed Sam Puckett.

Sam sounded embarrassed, reluctant. "Are you...uh... all right? Everything going all right over there?"

Good grief, Perdy thought in despair, did he think, as Ben had, that she wanted to be living with some man she hardly knew?

"Of course I'm all right," she replied shortly. "And no, everything else isn't all right. My house is full of his furniture. My furniture's in a storage warehouse in Indiana—and I don't know what to do about it. I don't know if I'm ever going to get to Cloverdale. Please, Sam—when are you going to get me out of this mess?"

"Perdita," he said carefully, as if edging his way around a pit of venomous adders. "I don't know what's going on over there with you two. Well, it's none of my business. You're a consenting adult and all—"

"*Nothing* is going on over here," she exclaimed in exasperation. "Don't talk like that, Sam."

"Perdita—" his voice became infinitely weary "—I don't like any of this. Something funny's going on. That lawyer, Algernon. He's trying to stall us."

She rubbed her fingertips between her eyebrows. "Stall? What do you mean?"

"Stall us. Purposely slow this down. I don't like it. All I can think of is that Squires has decided not to buy. He's just playing for time so he can hold you to the rent agreement."

Her heart almost stopped beating. Ben wasn't going to buy the house? Sam's words didn't seem like words at all; they seemed more like thick black clouds rolling across the sky, casting everything into an inescapable darkness.

"But why?" she asked in disbelief. "Why would he do that? He's already moved his things in."

"So he's a rich guy. He'll move them back out. What's a couple of thousand to him? The important thing, dear, is that he wanted your house for Christmas. And he's got it. In the meantime, Algernon's blocking every move I try to make to hurry up this sale. Once Christmas is over, or once Squires is ready, he'll split. Leaving you holding the bag. That's how it looks to me."

Perdy's head swam crazily. Was that all Ben had wanted in the first place? Her house for a few weeks so he could stare at his precious mountain and escape the rest of the world and the holiday he hated so much? What kind of ruthless and complicated game was he playing?

Sam had launched into one of his interminable and incomprehensible explanations about the gore area. All Perdy understood was that Algernon persisted that it be resolved in the hardest and most time-consuming and expensive way.

"He insists," Sam explained testily, "that we get a quit-claim deed from the guy who originally parceled off your lot."

"But that means finding somebody who sold it thirty years ago!" Perdy protested. "We might never find him!"

"I've already found him," Sam informed her dryly. "That's no problem. He's not going anywhere. He's been in the village cemetery for the past twelve years. The problem is we have to track down his heirs—six of them—and get them to sign the quitclaim deeds. Which isn't gonna be easy. You're going to need a lawyer to convince them they're not signing away a fortune in oil lands."

Her head began to throb unmercifully: more lawyer bills. "That could take months," she groaned.

"In the meantime, this Squires character has got you there, Perdita, and I hope you understand you're only there because he wants you there. Why he does isn't my business, but I'll tell you, dear, I wouldn't trust him."

Perdy was silent, trying to think clearly.

"You could have gone to court," Sam admonished her. "You could have blocked him and kept him out of there."

"I couldn't afford it, Sam! Mr. Small said it would be expensive, and I wasn't going to be chased out of my own house. You know that."

"Well, Squires could have gone to court, too," Sam replied darkly. "And he can afford it. He could have pulled the right strings and had you tossed into the street. But he didn't. Like I said, it's your life, dear, but you'd better realize you're in that house for one reason: he took no action against you, because he wants you there."

"But why?" Everything in her mind had jumbled together, as if a minor earthquake were taking place within her skull. It had never occurred to her that Ben could have taken her to court.

He wasn't going to buy the house. He was stalling. Yet he wanted her there. Why?

"Look," Sam warned. "I've been hearing a few things about this guy. Not nice things, either. Not at all. For one thing, he's a womanizer. Boston's blue-blooded version of Casanova. And I also hear he's always been the odd man out in his family—even if he did save that damned store."

She bit her lower lip. "Did you hear anything about him getting married?"

"Married?" Sam laughed derisively. "Him? Not too likely from what I hear—unless she's got a pile of stocks and bonds taller than the World Trade Center. The time he doesn't spend breaking hearts he spends building the family fortune. And he's built it pretty damned well."

So, she thought, her confusion slowly beginning to focus into anger: he was marrying for money. Perhaps that's why he showed so little tenderness to Cheryl. Maybe he didn't even mind taunting Cheryl with the hint he had another woman in the house.

The thought left a nasty taste in her mouth, the taste of squalor.

"I don't like any of it," Sam continued. "And I'm trying to tell you to be careful, all right? Don't get hurt or anything."

Don't get hurt. It was already too late for that, she thought bitterly. "What about my shop in Cloverdale?" she asked, her voice trembling. "Has somebody else bought it?"

"Not yet," Sam answered. "But, Perdita, the only good thing that may come out of this is that you have time to think over buying that place. I wish you'd reconsider. I'm worried for you on this Cloverdale nonsense, I really am."

"It's what I have to do," she said with more firmness than she felt.

When she hung up, she felt numb, addled. Everything was tumbling down around her. Only days ago she'd been sure she had her life in order, ready to start over on a sane course in Cloverdale. She had been sure she could handle Ben Squires. But she'd been miserably wrong on both counts. She wasn't even certain she should go to Cloverdale at all. But if not, where could she go?

She tried to distract herself by decorating the little tree. It didn't help. Even loaded with the crocheted ornaments, the tree looked scrawny. She stood studying it—the one touch of her in the room. It made sense that it looked inadequate, out of place.

She glanced coldly at Ben when he came downstairs. He had changed into tight-fitting black ski pants, boots, and a black turtleneck sweater.

"Ugliest tree I've ever seen," he said, black eyes settling on it with distaste. A muscle twitched in his cheek. Then he seemed to reach deeply inside himself, forcing his mood to change. "Think you can get used to furniture again?" The lightness in his tone sounded artificial.

She turned to face him, arms akimbo. "I want some things explained, mister! I just talked to Sam. He says you're trying to stall us. He says you're not going to buy this house at all. What's Algernon up to? What are you trying to pull?"

He coolly ignored her flashing brown eyes. He pushed up the sleeves of his sweater, exposing his strong wrists. "Sam's gone over the edge. I told you I intend to buy the house. And I do. Algie's doing what he does best—driving everybody crazy. But he's had one of his rare fits of lucidity.

Getting quitclaim deeds resolves this once and for all. No-body can ever bring up the gore area again. If you under-stood real estate, you'd know that."

"It's also the longest way to resolve it," Perdy accused, almost trembling with rage. "It could drag on—who knows how long? And Sam said you could have me evicted. Why haven't you?"

His dark eyes locked with hers, the muscle in his jaw twitching again. "I thought you might be rather recrea-tional. You're not. At least not in the way I'd hoped. But you can stay as long as you like. Maybe you'll change your mind."

He gave her his slow, crooked smile. She flushed, recall-ing Sam's insinuations. "I don't intend to change my mind. So why are you keeping me here? This could go on for months and months."

"Who knows?" he shrugged. "Maybe I'm doing it for your own good. Maybe I rather like you. I'm not used to people talking back to me. It's refreshing—in a perverse sort of way." He went to the closet and got his parka.

Perdy, her hands still on her hips, stamped her foot. "Where are you going? I said we have to talk."

He shrugged his wide shoulders again. They looked mas-sive in the parka. "For a snowmobile ride. The movers brought it. Want to come? I'll take you to the top of the mountain."

The light in his dark eyes told her that he wouldn't mind taking her to other, more sensual peaks, as well.

She shook her finger at him. "I don't want to go to the top of the mountain. I want some answers. Why don't you just buy the house, then get the deeds signed? You can af-ford it. I can't. You're the one who worries about that silly gore area—not me. And you're the one who wants to be here for Christmas—not me."

His cool gaze held her angry one. "Those deeds are your responsibility. You don't seem to know how to run your affairs. You need to learn. It appears I have to teach you."

She didn't like the insolence of his gaze or patronizing tone, or the way her heart was beginning to beat under the assault of those black eyes.

"After all," he said, one eyebrow taking on a satirical slant. "I'm not holding you prisoner—am I?"

But she was his prisoner, she thought. He had her trapped, and very neatly, too.

"Is this how you spend every Christmas? Ruining somebody's life?" she asked in despair.

"Oh, really," he said disgustedly. He turned his back to her and looked out the window at the mountain. "Leave Christmas out of it. I said I'm not up to anything. I said I'm buying the house. Sam Puckett is a paranoid old fussbudget and you're hysterical. I'm going up to the mountain. If you want to keep talking, you can come with me. Otherwise you can stay here and sulk."

He turned, his jaw set but his voice kinder. "Come on. You need to get out. You're upset about the furnace. And the van. And Sam—he doesn't know what he's talking about. I'm being honest with you, Perdy. I swear it."

Something in his expression stirred her, softened her. She wanted to believe him, to believe that nothing sinister was happening. Grudgingly she agreed to go with him. She did need to get out. Her head still hurt.

THE SNOWMOBILE, a sleek black and yellow Arctic Cat, droned like a great wintry wasp, and Perdy could feel its power vibrating against her jeaned thighs. Her long legs fitted neatly against Ben's, and her arms locked around his waist. She buried her face against the back of his parka, partly to shield her cheeks from the cold whip of the rushing air, and partly so she wouldn't be looking when they crashed into a tree or flew off the side of the mountain.

They skimmed the snowy pathway up the mountain, full speed, with Ben exulting in jumping icy hummocks and weaving crazily off the path between the pines. The coldness and the speed were exhilarating.

At last they reached the summit. Ben switched the engine off. The wind was biting and Perdy kept her face hidden against his back. "Are we still alive?" she asked.

He laughed. "I may have sacrificed a few ribs on the turns. You were squeezing tight. Is that how I get you to cling to me in passion? It's going to be damned awkward, making love on a speeding snowmobile."

She released her hold immediately, and with a swing of her long leg stepped off the snowmobile. Ben was beside her, his arm around her, drawing her close to shield her from the wind.

"Don't," she said, pushing his arm away, but he held her fast. She didn't trust herself in even his most casual embrace; he belonged to someone else. She had to keep reminding herself of that.

"It's no great thrill hugging you on those turns, you know," she muttered, her nose wrinkling in distaste. "Your coat still smells like Bummer."

He laughed, still holding her tightly, keeping himself between her and the lash of the wind. "I love it when you sweet-talk me," he drawled. "Why don't you flatter me like other women do? Tell me how wonderful I am and how pretty and green my money is?"

"I don't care about your pretty green money," she said, uneasy at his nearness.

"No," he answered, his breath pluming in the gray air. "I really don't think you do."

He looked out over the vista beneath them for a moment in silence. "Not a bad view, is it?" he finally asked, satisfaction in his voice.

She had to agree. Beneath them the small village of Mortimerford was set out like a model town for a train set, sparkling in the snow. The spires of the churches rose up against the gray sky, and the towered city hall looked like a small and cunningly made toy.

The Merrimac River, dark and tumbling, still unfrozen, coursed beneath an arching bridge, white wavelets tossing. Farther, beyond the little red general store, she could see the falls, where the black water tumbled in a foaming cascade. A few white gulls, lured from the coast, forty miles distant, cruised the air above the river, eyeing the rapids for fish.

Ben turned, his arm still holding her close. "There's the pond—you can just barely see it through the trees. And over there—" he pointed "—our house."

The little gray house with its dark red shutters looked toylike, too. Perdy felt somehow safe with Ben holding her so close, the bulk of his upper body shielding her from the wind. She had got an odd feeling when he'd said, "our house." The two words carried an intimacy that was startling, yet somehow comforting.

She looked up at him. Exhilaration glowed on his face, a light gleamed in the dark depths of his eyes. "This is the view I used to have from my room when I was a kid, staying here. This is where the cabin was. God, how I loved it here. In the winter we'd skate and ice-fish, and all summer long I roamed this place collecting everything—snakes, newts, turtles; even a baby porcupine once."

She had one of her peculiar, almost clairvoyant flashes. She could see him, young and lean and bronzed. She sensed the boy had been very different from the man; he had taken deep joy from life then.

"You remind me of her," he said against her ear.

"Who?" Perdy asked uncomfortably, feeling the fur of his parka tickle her cheek.

"The porcupine. She was young and lost and hurt and defenseless. They really are defenseless, you know, except for the prickles. She'd roll herself into a ball so all you could see were quills, but I finally tamed her."

Disturbed by his comparison, she studied the easy smile that curved his normally stern lips. "How long since you've been back here?" she asked, wanting to change the subject.

The smile went away, the light in his face dimmed. The familiar, cynical look returned. "Ten years. Ever since I took over Toynbee's. I was here ten years ago today, in fact. Right before Christmas. But I never came back. Till now."

She could feel the old anger, the old tension coursing through him. The wind bit at them sharply, and she let him hold her closer, sheltering her from the cold.

She stood, her back against his chest, feeling the warmth and strength of his arms around her. His face rested lightly next to hers, his chin on her shoulder.

This is how she wished it always could be, she realized. She liked this sense of closeness and comfort, the shared coziness that held off the cold of the rest of the world. She wished he were free and that she could trust him.

"How did you come to do it?" she asked, snuggling closer. "Take over Toynbee's, I mean? When you wanted to be a doctor?"

The wind gusted, a frigid flare, and she thought he wasn't going to answer. His voice was low, almost meditative. "The eldest son always takes over. I wasn't the eldest. I was merrily planning on following my uncle's humble footsteps and becoming an ordinary G.P.—a small-town doctor. But then, all of a sudden, I was the eldest. We're kind of like the Kennedy family. At least my mother liked to think so. And if one son falls, then the next picks up the pieces and carries on the business. Somebody had to. God forbid my family should ever go broke. Not one of them would know the first thing about earning a living. Oh, my youngest sister might. She does a lot of social work. I just wish she'd stop trying to use her theories on me."

Bitterness, not regret, seemed to edge his voice. She wished she could see him recapture that brief moment of sheer happiness he had experienced when they'd first reached the summit. "Will you ever go back to it? To medicine?" she probed.

"No. It's too late. Science went marching on without me. And Toynbee's gets into your blood. The complexities. The challenge. And the power. I didn't understand the lure of power then. I do now. I learned a great deal. Too much. I'm better off at Toynbee's than as a medic."

"Why?" The coldness she sensed building within him was more chilling than the wind assailing the peak.

"I would have got too emotionally involved with people to be a good doctor. I was that way, back then. Now all I want is a sensible life. I came back to see if it's too late for that, too. Maybe it isn't."

A sensible life, Perdy thought. That, too, was all she wanted. She felt his hands on her arms. He turned her toward him.

"Sometimes," he said, as if forcing himself to lighten his tone, "it's hard to have a sensible life. Especially when you get someone like Algie mixed up in it. He's another little family inheritance. An in-law. He's on the Toynbee payroll, but he can't really be trusted with any but the simplest tasks. Like arranging for me to buy a house. And you see where that's got us. He's always getting hung up on details, always nitpicking because it makes him feel important." He stared at her for a moment.

Suddenly his head dipped and before she knew what was happening, Ben had taken her face between his gloved hands and pressed his cold lips against her own.

It was a brief kiss, just long enough for it to reveal, then hide again, the warmth within.

He raised his head and stared down at her, his hands still touching her face. She stared back up at him, feeling strangely helpless. She was about to say he shouldn't have done it; she shouldn't have allowed it; he was, after all, engaged.

He laid a finger against her lips. "Tradition," he said casually. "You're always supposed to kiss a girl her first time on Miracle Mountain. Just a friendly tradition. That's all."

She stood still, looking up at him, but he stepped back slightly, his hands falling easily and finding his pockets, as if he'd already forgotten he'd touched her.

She shivered although she no longer felt the cold. She fought back the wish that he would kiss her again. What was wrong with her? One moment she would suspect he was a dark-hearted villain; the next, she was idiotically wishing to be in his arms.

"You look cold," he said, his voice not unkind. "Ready to go back?"

She nodded, turning to look down again at the little gray house with its dark red shutters. Their house. No. Her house. For a short time longer. It was the house he wanted for reasons she still could not quite fathom, the house where he was letting her stay, for reasons he alone knew.

He tugged at his black gloves, studying her. "Perdy, why are you working in that bar?"

She looked at him, startled. "Because I need the money."

A muscle worked in his jaw. "Is that why, really?"

She shivered. "Of course it's why." She shivered again.

He kept up his disturbing scrutiny. "Come on," he said. "You look like you're getting too cold."

He straddled the snowmobile, revved up its motor. She climbed on behind him, her legs fitting snugly behind his, her arms secure around his waist.

"Don't go so fast on the way down," she said, trying to lighten her own mood. "I want to get home in one piece."

"I'll be a veritable snail." He turned, tossing his dark hair off his forehead. "Trust me."

But he gunned the machine and they sped off with a skidding lurch. She felt both her heart and her stomach leap in fright. She squeezed her eyes shut and hid her face against his parka as they raced down in a breakneck descent.

Trust him, he had said.

She shut her eyes tighter, wishing she dared release him long enough to wipe her glove across her lips, to brush away the burning tingle of one short, meaningless kiss.

CHAPTER EIGHT

THE REST of their day together was maddeningly pleasant. The perfect gentleman, Ben tried to coax her into sharing his dinner of swordfish steak. He said he was concerned about her eating habits; she was worse than his preppie sister who subsisted on Häagen-Dazs ice cream and shrimp cocktail. Perdy refused, and dined on crackers and peanut butter.

The perfect gentleman, he shoveled the walk so she wouldn't have to wade through the snow to get to his car.

When the zipper on one of her good boots jammed, he fixed it, polite as could be. He insisted she wear his wool muffler. The windchill was becoming too brisk, he said, and she needed to protect her lungs.

He insisted, too, that she keep his electric blanket on her bed; now that his things had arrived, he had a down-filled comforter and didn't need it. She would.

The perfect gentleman, he drove her to work, walked her inside the lounge, and told her he would pick her up at quitting time. She protested that she had already made arrangements with another waitress for rides that week, but no, he insisted he would pick her up. He seemed bent on taking very good care of her. He acted absolutely protective, and it disturbed her, because she liked it.

If he weren't so gentlemanly, she brooded, she would know how to deal with him. She had met her share of would-be seducers, but none had broken through her defenses before. None had cared about her in the way Ben seemed to. None had evinced that strange and cold-blooded casualness Ben so often did.

The problem, she reflected, changing into her costume, was that she had met a man she didn't know how to handle. He was engaged, but he wanted her to live with him. He had made it clear he would like to make love to her, but when she refused, he accepted it as coolly as if she had turned down an invitation to play gin rummy. Although he seemed to be outrightly cruel and deceptive to Cheryl, he was putting Perdy off balance with unexpected kindnesses. He was an enigma, she decided. She couldn't understand him at all.

The lounge's happy hour kept Perdy on the run. She moved quickly and efficiently, dodging the occasional pinch or attempted pat on the bottom as expertly as a runner racing a familiar course of hurdles.

The customers grew louder as their drink tabs grew longer. The colored Christmas lights strung throughout the lounge did not really succeed in creating a holiday atmosphere, nor did the piano player, a thin, morose man whose repertoire alternated Christmas carols with soupy show tunes.

She let her tasks occupy the surface of her mind, but its depths were busily occupied with thoughts of Ben. She was obsessed with trying to link the jumbled pieces of Ben's situation together into a logical pattern. It was difficult, however, to be logical.

She believed that what Ben had told her so far was true. He had come back to Miracle Mountain to escape the pressures of Toynbee's. That was logical. But there was more. He had mentioned his brother. He had said that the eldest son always took over the business, and he had not always been the eldest.

His brother was dead; she was certain of that. He must have died ten years ago. Had he died at Christmastime? And

Ben had had to take over the reins of a failing Toynbee's and ride it, whipping all the way back onto the road of success.

But why had he wanted to come back now, before his marriage, as if he were trying to salvage something here? Why had he picked her house, out of all the houses in the area? It didn't make sense.

She tried to think, logically again. Did you ever notice any others houses for sale? No. Yours was the only one, and Ben made the rent agreement so he would be there for Christmas, as he had wanted. But was he really trying to stall the sale, as Sam had accused? Why had he allowed her to stay in the house, instead of forcing her out?

She thought hard about those questions. It was possible Ben was right. The gore area was a problem, and the safest way to eliminate it was the signing of the quitclaim deeds. As for letting her stay in the house, hadn't Sam said that Ben was a notorious womanizer? Everybody knew men were after just one thing, didn't they? All that was logical, wasn't it?

But, thought Perdy, what if he was trying to keep her there for other reasons? Could he really want something more than the purely physical from her? He did sometimes act with a gruff affection toward her. He really hadn't taken advantage of her—even when they'd slept in the same bed together those two nights.

Don't be a fool, she thought, trying to be logical again. Ben was not a nice man. He'd told her so himself. What would the scion of a wealthy family want with the daughter of an itinerant wrestler? Her background wasn't merely atypical, it was bizarre. Besides, he was getting married.

All right, she thought suddenly then, why was he getting married if he was such a notorious ladies' man? He certainly didn't act like a man in love. He was apparently wealthy enough that he didn't need to marry for money.

Heirs, her logical mind replied, as if it were obvious. Rich men want heirs. The rich marry the rich. Why should he love her? He's obviously incapable of loving anybody.

Okay, Perdy thought grimly, trying to back all this logic and reasoning against the wall and shake out the answers to some hard questions. What was she going to do? Why did her feelings toward him seesaw back and forth and flare so wildly?

Perhaps because she didn't know her own mind, she reasoned. She'd always run from involvement. She was scared. She had always believed the woman had to be the strong one, the way Esmeralda had been. She had spent that last year traveling around with poor Nels, trying to take care of him and too frightened to think of anything else. She was just catching up on some things . . .

Perdy suddenly realized that all the logic in the world wouldn't help her now. After all, what was she going to do? She'd gone and fallen in love with the man.

Love? her logical self scolded. *Don't you even think that word in my presence. I know what you want, you vixen! You desire him, that's all. Love is not possible between the two of you. Love indeed!*

Suddenly Perdy came back to herself. Her logical self had to be correct. How could she be in love with Ben Squires? A little shiver ran down her bare back, fluttered in her stomach. She felt dazed, a bit stunned. She was in love with him, and she knew it.

I'm standing in a bar in Manchester, New Hampshire, wearing a silly red costume with white rabbit fur. I am carrying a tray of martinis and practically talking to myself, because I've fallen in love with a gentleman who's no gentleman at all. He belongs to somebody else. I should have my head examined. How did this ever happen?

She was grateful when the holiday revelers in the lounge became so rowdy she could no longer think of anything else. Voices grew louder, almost drowning out the piano. The smoke thickened, the room began to feel smotheringly crowded.

One table, seating a group of rough-looking men, was becoming troublesome. Perdy saw Karen, who was trying to distribute drinks, get caught in an awkward embrace by one of the men while the others roared with laughter.

Karen extricated herself, nearly in tears. She was a weepy, excitable girl, not good in such situations. The manager, Larry, asked Perdy to take over Karen's tables—Perdy had already established herself as the girl who could handle the rough ones.

"Well, look what Santy Claus brung," the man who had grabbed Karen said, when Perdy delivered the drinks.

She didn't like his looks at all. He was huge. So were most of his friends and they all wore black leather jackets. He had a beard and long, unwashed hair pulled back into a dark, lank ponytail. He had a massive beer belly and a silver earring dangling from one ear.

He licked his thick lips. "The one with the legs. Those legs look like they go clear up to your neck, baby. Just how high do they go?"

He groped to feel her netted thigh, but she dodged him nimbly. "About twice as high as your IQ," she said, shooting him a deadly look.

The other men gave beery hoots of laughter, but he did not. She could feel his angry eyes follow her as she left the table. All those years in the company of the hard-talking wrestling crowd had made her wary. She hoped she hadn't misjudged him. He might very well be meaner than she had thought—perhaps she should have been less sharp with him. She tried to put him out of her mind.

The lounge grew even more crowded and more stifling. She scurried madly, trying to keep up with everything. She wished she'd eaten more; she was having spells of light-headedness. She was relieved when most of the rough-looking men left. But the burly man with the ponytail stayed, and he kept staring at her.

"Gimme another," he slurred out as she passed his table. She ignored him, but on her way back, he reached out, grabbing her arm. The floor was too congested for her to elude him.

"I said gimme another rye," he ordered, yanking her close to him, his breath hot in her face. "And stop actin' so stuck up. Or I'll make you sorry."

She didn't try to struggle. She put her free hand on her hip and stared down at him as if he were a large but harmless insect. "You've have enough to drink, friend. And the law says I don't have to serve you anymore when you reach that point."

He gripped her arm more tightly. "Who's gonna stop me, baby? You? You wanna fight? Good. I like it better when they fight. I like it a whole lot. Especially when they're as pretty as you. Go ahead. Try and hurt me, doll-baby."

He jerked her onto his lap with a surprisingly fast movement for a man so massive. "Go ahead," he breathed in her face. "Try to fight me, Legs."

"You asked for it," she replied evenly. With a lightning stroke she shot her elbow hard against his collarbone, as Mr. Kim had taught her to, many years before.

He moaned with pain and cursed with rage. Perdy sprang from his hold and fled to the manager, who gave the high sign to Moose, the bouncer. Moose, accompanied by Alvin, the biggest bartender, hustled the man to the door.

The troublemaker didn't put up much of a struggle, but he threw a scowl back over his shoulder at Perdy, who had taken refuge behind the bar. She had another of her nervous feelings of foreboding. The man was a coward and she knew cowards were always the most dangerous.

Once he was ejected, she made her way back onto the floor where she collided with a tall, hard body. Her heart seemed to turn into a butterfly that flew into her throat, wings beating violently. It was Ben, and his expression was anything but gentlemanly.

His black-gloved hands were on her bare shoulders. "I came just in time to witness that little drama," he said acidly, nodding toward the door the man had just been taken through. "How many times a night does an ape like that try to maul you?" His lean face was tense with suppressed fury.

She tried to chase the butterfly out of her throat. "He was the first," she retorted, more disturbed by him than by the incident with the drunk. "He just happened to be slower at taking hints than most."

"Dammit!" He shook his head, his straight brows drawn together. "Are you all right?"

"Of course I'm all right," she said, embarrassed at the turmoil his nearness was creating in her. "I'm used to this kind of thing. What are you doing here? It isn't closing time yet."

"You're used to this kind of thing, are you? Good Lord, just what kind of life have you led?"

"Not your kind, obviously," she said, stung by his criticism.

"Obviously," he said. His hands fell away from her. She felt as if he'd dropped an invisible wall between them. "I came in early because I felt like a drink," he said, his expression unreadable.

He stood staring down at her a moment, then eased his way through the crowd and took a seat at the bar.

For the next hour he nursed a scotch and water, and Perdy could feel his eyes on her every move. He was angry about something. It was more than the scene with the drunk; she could feel it. He hadn't come to the lounge for a drink. He had better liquor at home.

She was grateful but apprehensive at quitting time. She was still worried about why he had come early, why he had watched her so carefully. She was too emotionally drained for another confrontation with Ben. As she changed out of her costume, she offered up a silent prayer of thanks that the furnace was repaired and he had his own bed. She felt far too vulnerable to spend another night in his arms.

When Perdy re-entered the lounge, Ben wasn't there.

"Your boyfriend went to get his car," Karen said. "The lot was so crowded he had to park on a side street. He said to wait in here for him. And, Perdy—he's gorgeous! Where'd you ever find him?"

Perdy gave her a cryptic smile, but didn't answer. It would have been too difficult to explain that Ben wasn't her "boyfriend," that he was just the man she happened to be living with.

Karen left. Only Larry, the manager, remained. The empty lounge, its cheerless Christmas lights now dimmed, seemed oppressive, its air stale and smoky. She stepped out the side door for a moment to clear her head, breathe some fresh air, and wait for Ben.

The narrow street was dark, empty, and the wind began to chill her. She pulled Ben's muffler more tightly around her chin and began to pace, half from the cold, half from restlessness.

Suddenly, from the shadows of another doorway, a figure appeared, lurching toward her. It was the drunk who had grabbed her earlier. He lunged at her.

"Come on, baby. We're goin' for a ride. I'm gonna see just how long those legs are."

Large arms tried to pick her up. She saw the flash of something gleaming in his hand. She veered deftly, but felt one of the metal studs of his leather jacket graze her cheek. He was between her and the door of the lounge now, and instinctively she had backed into the circle of light from the streetlamp.

She threw her right arm out, as if for balance, her left hand taking her heavy shoulder bag by the strap to hold it and use as either shield or weapon.

The big man edged toward her, his legs not fully steady. "Still like to fight, huh? Good. I told you—I like it when they fight. But you won't feel like fighting when I'm through with you."

A car was coming down the street, its lights carving slices through the darkness. The man paused, eyeing her. She was uncertain whether to run or stand her ground. She had defended herself more than once, but there was a primal meanness in this man that made her very nervous.

Then the car slid silently to the curb beside them, stopping. Perdy gasped with relief when Ben leaped out.

"Watch out," she cried, warning him.

Ben didn't even glance at her. He vaulted toward her attacker, threw a shoulder block to the man's midsection, pulled back immediately, then delivered a precise and driving uppercut to the man's jaw. The drunk groaned, staggered, then sagged, his back sliding down the brick wall of the building to slump, unconscious, against it.

Ben grimaced, stripped off his right glove, and rubbed his fist. "I hope," he said, casting her a dark look, "that you didn't mind that for once in the history of our relationship, I did the hitting."

She ran up beside him. "Hit him again," she cried, raising her purse to swat the drunk on the head.

Ben seized her arm, restraining her, his other arm catching her around the waist. "Perdy," he said softly, his face close to hers, "stop. He's already unconscious. He'll be out for a good fifteen minutes. And you're hurt. Did he cut you?"

She stared up at him, trembling. Her emotions were staging a small riot within her. He touched the scratch on her cheek. His knuckles were already turning dark with bruises.

"You're hurt, too," she said, examining his hand. "Oh, your poor hand!" She squeezed it in concern and without thinking pressed it against her cheek.

"Ouch," he gritted out. "Don't. Here. You're shaking." He drew her close, one arm holding her tightly to him, his injured hand still touching her face. His fingers were warm against her cheek. "Don't worry," he said, kissing the top of her head. "I'll live to play Tchaikovsky again. Just maybe not this week. Here, get in the car."

Once inside, he took her in his arms again. She held him tightly, unthinkingly, her cheek against his chest. He kissed her head again. "Sure you're all right?"

"Yes. Yes." Still trembling, she raised her face to his.

He kissed her, a long, possessive kiss, one that was tender yet hungry. He kissed her cheek, her ear, the silky skin at her temple near the corner of her eye. His lips pressed against her brows, her lashes, then claimed her mouth again.

His hand tunneled beneath her jacket, caressing her back, her side, then came to rest on her breast. He caressed it gently, then his hand moved to the other one.

"You're really all still here?" he asked, laughing between his gasps. "Every bit of you?"

She pressed more closely to him, loving the touch of his hand as it ran, gentle, searching, across the front of her sweater. "Yes. All here." She stretched up and kissed the curve of his lean jaw.

He kissed her again, until she felt almost faint. "Perdy," he said, his arms around her again, his breathing still labored. "Does it occur to you that suddenly we're both feeling very affectionate toward each other?"

"Yes," she whispered shakily, and kissed his jaw again. He drew back from her slightly, holding her by the upper arms, staring into her eyes. "Did you know he had a knife?" His face looked pained with concern.

She nodded again. She wished only that he'd kiss her again. He seemed to be trembling slightly himself—whether with cold or emotion, she did not know.

He sank his teeth into his lower lip in frustration, still staring at her. "If you knew, why did you just stand there?

Why didn't you run? Scream? Try to flag down the car when you saw it coming? And I left word for you to stay inside, dammit! What were you doing out here?"

"I needed some air. And I was trying to decide the best thing to do—run or fight him off. When you came up, I was—uh—thinking." She seemed unable to recover her breath.

"You were thinking?" he chided her in disbelief. "Oh, Perdy. You're the most impossible, improbable creature I've ever met. And you're making me forget that I'm extremely mad at you." Perdy was silent. "Wait here, and keep the doors locked. Right now I'm going to drag our friend inside the lounge, and call the police. Then we've got to talk, Perdy. I've got a few things to say to you."

He touched her cut cheek again, gently, his black eyes losing themselves in hers. "Idiot," he said, and kissed her again.

AN HOUR AND A HALF LATER she and Ben were sitting in an all-night doughnut shop. "What are we doing here?" she asked wearily. "It seemed like we spent hours at the police station. It's almost three o'clock in the morning. I want to go to sleep."

Ben flexed his bruised hand and cradled his coffee cup with the other. "I told you we have to talk. This isn't exactly a typical evening for me, either. I start out at a dive named Mr. Pongo's, progress to a street fight in defense of a sassy barmaid, and end up in the Manchester Police Station, giving a statement to a detective who looks like he eats barbells for breakfast. Ergo, like any good Yankee under duress, I need a doughnut."

Perdy stared at hers, untouched on its napkin, with disinterest. She didn't like being called a sassy barmaid. She wished Ben would act the way he had in those few moments outside the lounge—when he had held her as if he really cared for her. He seemed to have reverted to his usual cold-blooded self.

"You need to eat something," he said gruffly. "Besides, I wanted to get you in a public place—to make sure you behave. Because you're not going to like everything I'm going to talk about."

She pushed the doughnut away. His face had that distant look again, as if he were deliberately shutting her out. She could sense anger rising in him again.

The edge of his mouth curled, as if he were about to say something unpleasant. The fluorescent lights of the shop made his high cheekbones seem sharper, harder.

"While you were at work tonight, I went through your papers. Everything. Your contracts on the house, on the business in Cloverdale. Your checkbook. Your bankbook. All those things you left lying so conveniently on your dresser."

His black eyes never left her face. She stiffened, her fatigue suddenly erased. Disbelief and anger rushed through her system like wildfire. "You what? You had no right—"

Her right fist automatically clenched in anger, but he covered it with his bruised hand. "Be quiet. Keep your voice down. I said you wouldn't like it."

He set his jaw. "You're in trouble. Big financial trouble. If you listen to me, you just might escape. So sit there, and for once in your life, don't talk back to me."

The hand that clenched her fist was as ironlike as his gaze.

"What do you have besides the house and the furniture in Cloverdale? And your van and those expensive clothes on your back?"

She glared at him, wanting to pull her hand away, but she stayed still, as if his grip welded them together.

"Answer me," he ordered. His hands tightened around hers. She stared down at his darkened knuckles.

She held her chin high. "A very good sewing machine. My clothes aren't expensive. I make them."

"Well, my tall, beautiful clotheshorse, do you know just how precarious your finances are?" he demanded. "Do you have any idea?"

She tossed her head. "Of course. I told you a hundred times I couldn't afford this—this stupid gore-area mess. I told you!"

He stared at her in disbelief. "You really couldn't afford to move out, could you? I thought you were fooling around—having a bit of fun with me. You weren't, were you?"

With her free hand, she slapped the surface of the table in irritation. He caught her hand in his other one, lacing his fingers through hers as if in affection, but his grasp was tight.

"Just explain one thing," he said, his voice low. "The expensive bracelet. That threw me off about you from the beginning."

"What bracelet?" she asked truculently. "What are you talking about?"

"The snake bracelet," he returned, still holding both her hands tightly. "The one you always wear."

"That thing? It's not worth anything," she said in confusion. "Esmeralda got it in a box of things we bought at an auction once. She kept it because it was unusual."

He shook his head in disbelief, the line of his mouth harsh. "Perdy, the thing's real gold. It must be worth a thousand dollars. It's an antique. You mean to tell me you didn't even know that? How could I believe you were broke when you dress the way you do and were sporting a thing like that?"

"How am I supposed to know what real gold looks like?" she asked, trying to hold back the tears. He had his fingers laced so tightly through hers that it hurt. "I kept it because it was Esmeralda's, that's all. Let go of me. You're hurting me."

Perdy's head reeled—the bracelet was worth a thousand dollars? That practically meant she was rich. She hadn't even known. No wonder he suspected she had "admirers."

He didn't let go. "I didn't believe you," he said, his eyes boring into hers. "Not until I saw you actually working in that dive last night. I thought you were eating peanut butter because you were a junk food addict or something, not because your back was against the wall. Then I looked through your papers."

With a sudden movement he released her hands, reached inside his jacket and drew out a sheaf of papers. "This is the offer you signed for the business in Cloverdale. Did you even read it?"

He threw the papers on the table between them. "You signed to buy everything 'as is'. The people selling to you are responsible for nothing—not one thing. Then I talked to Sam Puckett. Perdy, you haven't even seen this place. How could you be such a fool?"

She snatched the papers up, stuffing them into her purse. "It's none of your business, or Sam Puckett's either. He shouldn't be telling you anything about me. You're both beneath contempt."

One of his straight brows rose cynically. "When I saw that parody of a contract, I went straight to him. I've shaken far more important information out of far tougher men than he, my dear. You can be assured of that."

Ben took a sip of coffee, frowned, and set the cup back down with a sharp sound. "He told me you have this bee in your bonnet about buying a business you've never seen in a town you don't even know. That you were so eager to do it, you'd sign anything. And you certainly did. You don't even know what you bought, woman! The business may have failed. The building may be falling down—"

"If it failed, I'll make it work," she insisted, blinking back tears. "If it's falling down, I'll prop it back up. If I need more money, I'll sell the bracelet. A thousand dollars

s a lot of money. And I'm going to Cloverdale because it's
ny home. I've never belonged anywhere, but I'll belong
here. I feel it!''

He seized her wrist, pinning it to the table. "A thousand
ollars isn't a lot of money. A business can eat a thousand
ollars in one bite. Perdy, you don't buy businesses on a
eeling. On feeling you fall in love or some foolish thing like
hat, but you don't buy a business. Have you ever run a
usiness?''

She turned her eyes away, staring stubbornly at the rows
f stupid doughnuts behind the counter. They seemed to
tare back, like angry, empty eyes. She bit her lip.

"Answer me! Or I'll tie you up in legal problems so
ghtly you'll never go to Cloverdale or anyplace else. Tell
e the truth, or I'll have you wrapped up in legalities the
vay spiders wrap a fly. Did you ever run a business?''

She stared at the doughnuts. She bit her lip again. The
oughnuts stared back. "No. I've never run a business."

"How did you ever get into this situation? How did you
nd up in New Hampshire with a house and nothing else?
Vhere did you come from? What did you do?''

She thought dazedly of spiders wrapping up a struggling
ly. "The woman who raised me left me the house. Esmer-
lda. I told you that. And a little money. I needed most of
to pay off my father's funeral bills. I'd been taking care
f him."

"Where?'' His voice kept digging into her like a sur-
eon's scalpel.

"All over. We just sort of rambled. The Southwest. He
as sick, and scared. It helped him to keep moving."

She could feel his eyes burning into hers. He threw an old,
eamed envelope on the table between them. "And who are
ese people?''

She stared down, her anger escalating. The envelope was
ull of snapshots. She had found them, cleaning out Es-
eralda's dresser drawers. He had no right looking at them.

He dumped the contents out, fanning the snapshot across the Formica tabletop. "I said who are they? Thi guy—the Adonis in the silly cape."

She looked, blinking hard again to keep back the tears. The picture was an old one. It was Nels, in his halcyon day as the Black Viking.

"My father. And he wasn't silly." Her voice was bitter but sounded somehow distant to her.

"And who is this—creature?" His voice was as edge with bitterness as hers.

Her eyes moved to another snapshot of Nels, making ferocious face at the camera. "That's my father, too. Af terward. He had an accident. He was burned."

"My God, Perdy," he said, his voice unbelieving. "M God. That's who you were taking care of?"

She studied the picture, her vision clouding. Nels's once handsome face was ravaged. To a stranger's eyes it was monster's face—she knew that all too well. But she had loved him more because of the suffering he had survived She had fought hard to protect him from people's revulsio and scorn.

"And who are these people—including the funny-lookin, kid?" She looked, her heart beating high in her chest thudding hard against her breastbone. It was an old Christ mas picture, taken in the trailer. In the background, sh could see the tree. In the foreground, she stood betwee Frankie and Esmeralda, holding her Christmas present, portable sewing machine. She was eleven years old an looked all knobby-kneed, with big glasses and braces on he grinning teeth. She was already taller than either Esmer alda or Frankie.

"The funny-looking kid is me," she said between he teeth. "That's Frankie and Esmeralda. They were like par ents to me."

She stared at the photo. Frankie was laughing, waggin his large cigar at the camera. Esmeralda was mugging flir atiously, her green eyes twinkling. She looked very beautiful.

There were other pictures taken when Perdy was older—one of her dramatically modeling some new creation for the benefit of Esmeralda's camera. There was a funny one of Perdy pretending to have Hugo the Horrible in a headlock, and another of diminutive, muscular Mr. Kim hoisting her into the air as she feigned terror. There was another of her standing with Frankie and Esmeralda and Tiny Terrible Waldo, another midget, and Frankie's former tag-team partner.

"What did you do?" Ben asked, frowning at her as she shuffled through the pictures. "Grow up in a goddam circus?"

His words stung. As she lifted her face, she could feel the hatred glittering in her eyes. He was mocking the people she'd loved most in her life, people to whom the world had not been kind. "Yes," she hissed, her upper lip curled. "In the circus. With the rest of the freaks. Not everybody's blood is blue—you bastard."

He glanced at the pictures dispassionately, gathered them up and thrust them back into the envelope. He handed it to her. "I'm sorry, Perdy. It was just a surprise. I didn't mean it the way it sounded."

She snatched the envelope away and put it into her purse. Contempt for him flooded through her, making her head pound. "If you're through with me, will you please take me home? And then stay out of my way? Because I hate the sight of you. I really do."

He lifted his coffee cup, watching her as she tried to struggle into her jacket.

"I said I was sorry. And I am—deeply. I didn't understand, and I didn't mean to hurt you. But I'm not through with you. I told you Cloverdale's got disaster written all over it, in letters a mile high. But I can help you. I've got a much better business proposition for you."

She tossed him a hot-blooded glance. "I don't want anything from you. Ever."

His black eyes read her brown ones, disregarded the message, then settled on her lips. "You haven't heard the offer."

"I don't want to." She pulled on her gloves as if they were gauntlets.

He sipped at his coffee. "But it's interesting. And mutually beneficial." He regarded her over the edge of his mug. A smile toyed at the edge of his mouth.

"I'd like to take care of you. I'd like you to be my mistress," he offered, as casually as if he were offering her another cup of coffee.

She sprang up from her seat, breathing hard. She felt the most violent flood of emotions she had ever experienced in her life. She seemed to see two of him, and she was going to kill them both. She opened her mouth to tell him she didn't want to be the mistress of any man—least of all an engaged one, but the words wouldn't come out.

Someone had stolen her voice. She looked wildly around the shop. All the doughnuts were staring at her again. One winked. It winked again. Then they all began to wink. They winked and winked and winked.

Then, for the first time in her life, she fainted.

CHAPTER NINE

"THAT," GROWLED BEN, kissing the back of her neck, "was the most Victorian thing I've ever seen in my life. I make a friendly indecent proposition, and you swoon. Actually swoon. Oh, stop pretending. I know you're awake."

She wriggled away, burying her head under the pillow. He had made her sleep in his bed because it was more comfortable. He had taken hers. She was not only awake, but still reeling with embarrassment at having fainted in a doughnut shop, of all places.

"I said stop pretending. I brought you breakfast. You've got to eat. Dr. Squires's orders."

He pried her fingers loose from the pillow and lifted it away. He plumped it up and set it against the oak headboard, settling a second pillow on top of it. "Come on," he instructed, patting the pillows. "Sit. Eat. Up and at 'em."

Perdy sighed. "Go away. Then I'll eat. I don't want to have to look at your face."

He gently lifted her, forcing her to sit against the pillows. "I'll see that you eat. And it's your face you're worried about, not mine. I know your mind by now. You haven't got your makeup on so you think you're naked. Well, I like your naked face. You're much prettier without all that war paint."

"Here," he said, handing her her glasses. "Try these. Don't worry. I'll never tell a soul I saw you like this. Your dark secret is safe with me."

She snatched her glasses and thrust them on, then stared at the tray in disgust. "What is it exactly, that you do to eggs," she demanded, "that makes them turn green and brown like that?"

He laughed. "On the road to recovery, I see. Your formidable line of defense is falling back into place. How prim you look—with your high-necked nightgown, your scrubbed face, your big glasses. In spite of the front you put on, you're a prude at heart. Who would have suspected it?"

She took an experimental taste of the eggs, a careful nibble of the toast. Both tasted horrible and wonderful at the same time. She was starved.

He was studying her carefully, a smile on his mouth. "I owe you an apology," he stated calmly. "I should have seen you were getting woozy. Unobservant of me. But I was intent on getting to the truth of the matter."

She finished another forkful of rubbery eggs. "You owe me an apology all right." She cast him a murderous glance. "For snooping in my personal papers. For pawing through my private family photographs. For insulting my family, and then having the gall to think I'd be interested in being your—"

She couldn't say the word mistress. Instead, she gave a shudder of revulsion that she hoped was sufficiently damaging to his ego. He had wounded her deeply; she wanted to hurt him back.

He shrugged noncommittally. "My timing's been better. But I don't go around making that proposition to women every day. In fact, it's the first time I've ever made it. And stop pretending you hate me. You don't. I remember how you kissed me outside the lounge."

"Oh, pooh." She bit off another piece of brittle toast. "I'd have kissed Godzilla if he'd punched out that lunk for me."

"You haven't had your coffee. I forgot how utterly vile you are in the morning. Drink up. Then we'll talk."

She gave him another poisonous look. "We've got nothing to talk about. And wipe that smirk off your face. It's Christmas Eve tonight. Shouldn't you be out knocking over snowmen or strangling reindeer or something?"

Suddenly his black eyes got that faraway look. He watched her sip her coffee. His cool smile remained, as if frozen on his face. "How odd. I forgot. All I was thinking of was you. So it's Christmas Eve. Amazing."

She finished her coffee and he poured her another cup from a silver pot on the tray. She finished her eggs and toast, avoided a sausage, and drank her orange juice.

He was still watching her, and it gave her a curious, familiar sensation in the pit of her stomach. Something in his eyes had changed, but she couldn't read what secrets he held in those ebony depths.

"Let's not talk about my quirks and psychological shortcomings," he said, forcing the tightness out of his smile. "Let's talk about yours. You've got to get this Cloverdale business out of your head, Perdy. To put it in psychological jargon, you've been indulging in magical thinking. You've convinced yourself that all will be sweetness and light in Cloverdale—when you get there, something magic will happen, you'll never have problems again. But there won't be any magic. The world will still be the world, you'll still be you, and you'll discover you haven't found paradise at all. You'll discover just the opposite—a new kind of hell."

Her back stiffened against the pillows. She took another sip of coffee. It was, she thought irrelevantly, as black and strong and addictive as his eyes. "You haven't the foggiest notion," she said. "My instincts might just be better than your logic. It's my life and I know what I want to do with it."

"I have a very clear notion," he corrected. He filled her coffee cup again. "Hold this," he said, pressing the cup back into her hands. He lifted the tray from her lap and set it back on the antique night table.

"You can't go to Cloverdale." He spoke slowly and distinctly, as if he were speaking to a child. "The building's in a shambles. The business can't possibly make it. As I told you before, you'd lose your shirt. And maybe even your high-necked nightgown. I know. I had Algie check it out."

Her fingers tightened around the china cup. She pushed her glasses more firmly onto her nose, and stared at him in irate disbelief. She set the coffee cup down on the night table with a sharp rap. "You did what?"

He nodded curtly, his eyes holding hers. "I sent Algie to Cloverdale. Last night, after I went through your papers. I talked to him a short time ago. And don't worry that I ruined his Christmas. He's already winging his way back to Boston, happy as a lark he's been able to report such bad news."

"I don't believe you," she said, folding her arms protectively across her breasts. "You're lying."

He followed her movement with interest, lifting his dark brows. "I'm not lying. I was concerned. The longer I've known you, the more concerned I've become. And for all Algie's faults, he's thorough. Do you want to know what he found out?"

"No!" she said sharply. She had a sudden, desperate desire not to hear what he was going to say next. She knew his words were going to bring an end to something; to a dream—perhaps a foolish dream—but the only one she had.

"You're going to hear it anyway. Your property is a ninety-year-old building with plumbing problems. The place needs a new furnace, and there's extensive water damage from a leaky roof. There's termite damage. The inventory is damaged—the fabrics themselves are mildewy. You'd be up to your pretty neck in debt for repairs. And you agreed to pay the asking price, which is about twice what the dump is worth. The seller in Cloverdale was waiting for a sucker, and you practically walked into his open arms. That's your dream shop. That's where your magical thinking would have led you."

Perdy felt her jaw trembling, and she tried to set it firmly. She was reminded of the time, as a child, when her little mongrel dog ran into the traffic and was killed. Frankie had told her the dog was dead, and she had knelt by its little body, saying "No! He isn't dead! He isn't!" She had cried and cried then, but she didn't want to cry now—not in front of Ben. Instinctively she knew he was telling the truth, and all the denial in the world wouldn't change it.

She tried to stop trembling. "Is that all?" she asked, her voice shaky. His every word had been like a nail driven into her heart. "Does it also have hot and cold running rats? Poison spiders? Or better yet—a gore area?"

He put his hand under her chin. She tried to turn her face away, but he wouldn't let her. "Yes, Perdy. There's more. And I didn't do this to hurt you. I did it because I—rather—care for you. I didn't want you jumping out of the frying pan into the fire. I know what it's like to walk in and try to bring a dying business back to life. It can break your back and put calluses on your heart. It can ruin you. I'd like to spare you that."

"Your concern is touching," she said, folding her arms tighter. She couldn't keep the wobble out of her voice, and she wished he wasn't touching her. She liked his touch, and he was more dangerous to her than Cloverdale could ever be. "What else? Tell all. You're really making this a great Christmas, you know that?"

His fingers still held her chin, their touch gentle. "The rest is that even if the building was in perfect shape and you had a great inventory, you'd never make it, Perdy. The shop's tiny. It went out of business because a far better fabric shop opened three years ago in a nearby mall. It's an established chain store, nationwide. You couldn't compete. Ever."

She bit her lip. She felt cold and empty. Worse, she felt foolish and betrayed. Some deeper, more rational level of her mind had always feared that her idea of a perfect life in Cloverdale was a mirage, nothing more. Its lure had kept her moving desperately—toward the dream. But as the dream began approaching reality, it wavered, it shimmered sinisterly, it disappeared. It was gone.

Tears rested on her lower lashes. She tried to blink them back. She could not. They spilled over, trailing hotly down her cheeks.

"I'm sorry," he repeated. He took off her glasses, very gently, and wiped the tears away with his hand. "I didn't want to hurt you. It was the last thing I wanted. But Cloverdale would have hurt you more. And you see, there's no reason to go there now."

"No," she said, squaring her shoulders. The room was a blur, and she could see nothing clearly except him, and even he was dim through the tears she still struggled to hold back. She felt as if she had a hot stone lodged in her throat. "I don't have any reason to go there. Sam was right. Everybody was right. Great."

He set her glasses on the night table beside the tray. He took the coffee cup from her hands because she was trembling so hard she was almost spilling it. His hard face looked torn with inarticulate sympathy, and that only made things worse. She couldn't look at him.

"So," he muttered. "You knew it, deep down, all along, didn't you?"

She stayed silent, trying to swallow the stone in her throat. Had hope, mere hope, been such a stupid thing? Her weary conclusion was that it had.

"So," he repeated. He put his hands on either side of her face. "Why don't you stay here with me? I'll buy the house, but you stay here. I'd be here every weekend. Or you could come to Boston, where we'd have even more time. We could use this place as a retreat—to get away from everything. I'll invest your money from the house sale for you, so you'll always have some security. If you want a shop, I'll buy you one, anywhere—Manchester, Boston—it doesn't matter. But you shouldn't be selling fabric, you should be designing. I could give you your own boutique in Toynbee's. Toynbee's is so stuffy it could use a touch like yours. What do you say?''

She didn't say anything. She turned her face away sharply from his touch. She grabbed one of the extra pillows and hugged it to her, rolling over on her side so she didn't have to see him. She blinked hard, then squeezed her eyes shut and hugged the pillow tighter.

"Just leave me alone," she said at last, dully. It was like last night all over, and she was too tired to fight. What kind of man was he, trying to take a mistress practically on the eve of his wedding? And what kind of woman was she, to love him in spite of it? Suddenly she missed Esmeralda more than ever.

She felt his hand on her arm, its warmth penetrating the flowing fabric of her sleeve. "If you're worried about your future," he said gruffly, "don't be. We can draw up a contract. I'll make sure you're always taken care of."

She gave a bitter laugh against the pillow. "I've signed enough contracts to last me a lifetime, thanks. And you seem to forget—it was the house, not me, that was for sale. And you also forget that I hate you. Which I really do."

She lay there, clutching the pillow, feeling cold and empty. He'd give her a contract—a contract! Of all the cold-blooded men she'd ever met in her life, he took top honors. He laid it all out as neatly as a business proposition, which, she supposed, was all it meant to him. He hadn't said he loved her or needed her or even bothered to ask if she cared for him.

His gravelly voice was careful and controlled. "We get along, Perdy, even when we argue. Haven't you noticed that? How many people can argue and have fun at the same

time? You challenge me. I don't think you'd back down for
the devil himself. Most women get wind of my money and
simper like lapdogs. You couldn't simper if you tried.
You're ready to take on the whole world with nothing more
than a sense of style, a fast answer, and your mascara. You
amuse me. You make me forget the dark side of things."

She took her face away from the pillow long enough to
shoot him a killing glance. "I amuse you! How nice! I
doubt, however, if I'll amuse Cheryl. She seems to be one
of the things you're forgetting! So just stop this—this farce!
Don't you remember you're planning to walk her down the
aisle?" Angry and humiliated, she squeezed her eyes shut
and pressed her face into the pillow again, as if to erase his
presence.

"Cheryl?" he rasped, amazement in his voice. "What's
Cheryl got to do with this? Yes, I'm walking her down the
aisle—to give her away."

Her eyes popped open. She raised herself on her elbow
and turned to stare at him. "To give her away?"

"Yes," he said, frowning down at her impatiently. "She's
my youngest sister. Cheryl the Preppie Peril. The sweet little addlepate out to reform the world—so long as it doesn't
interfere too much with her wedding, which she intends to
be the wedding of the century. Even though she knows I hate
weddings."

"Cheryl is your *sister*?" she asked in disbelief. Her heart
started to beat faster. He wasn't engaged? She didn't know
if that made things less complicated, or more.

He studied her, one eyebrow rising in a combination of
consternation and amusement. "Who did you think Cheryl
was?"

"Your fiancée," she said, her eyes holding his gaze. He
put his hand on her shoulder, and it seemed to burn through
her nervous system.

He laughed. "Cheryl? Where did you get such a ridiculous idea?" He shook his head. All the amusement left his

face. "No wonder you've played so hard to get. You really are a confirmed moralist, aren't you? What a rarity. A woman who doesn't want to want somebody else's man. But I'm not somebody else's man. I just want you to be my woman."

His hand moved slowly down her arm, stroked the fine bones of her wrist, the sensitive skin over her pulse. He frowned. "But I'll be honest. You have to understand that I never intend to marry again. Never. I'll make that clear from the start. I won't marry you—or anyone else. This arrangement of ours is as close to anything permanent as I intend to get. But I'll see that you're kept comfortably. Very comfortably."

Her eyes widened. Marry again? This was the first time he'd ever mentioned being married. He wanted no more permanent relationships—just neat, contractual ones. Maybe that's why Ben kept Algie around; he was probably an expert on "mistress" contracts.

"Don't pretend you don't care for me, Perdy," he murmured, bending nearer, his voice low. "Don't even try. The night I walked in here, something happened. We both know it. Our spirits called to one another. And our bodies. That's what those strange songs are singing inside of us. It's why my flesh dances when it touches yours. You answer something in me and I in you. And we've known it from the start."

She shivered as she felt him fling away the cream-colored overlet, the blue satin top sheet. His body was on the bed now, full length, pressed against her in the same maddening proximity as when they had slept together. His hand was moving up and down her arm in a slow and sensual caress.

His lips were on the nape of her neck, hot, gentle, moist, and she felt the tracing of his tongue as it moved to the lobe of her ear. She lay still a moment, her body aching with awakening desire.

She couldn't stand this any longer, she thought in panic.
Now that she knew he didn't belong to another woman, she
couldn't resist him, yet she had to. She loved him, but he
didn't love her. What he was offering her was everything she
had been raised to scorn, to flee from.

She sprang away, scrambling to her hands and knees in
the bed, the tangle of satin sheets around her. Almost lazily
he reached out for her, and as she knelt, trembling there,
and he wrapped his arms around her, she had no more
strength to resist. He drew her down, helpless, to rest against
the hardness of his chest. His mouth claimed hers as if it
were some sort of rich inheritance he had been waiting too
long for. He kissed her with a completeness and a passion
that seemed inevitable.

Half-reluctantly, half-desirous, she let her hands rest on
his shoulders, her lips yield to his. She hardly protested
when he hastily undid the buttons of her gown, sliding the
fabric from her shoulders, her arms, so that it sank in a bile
low around her bare waist.

He was right, she thought desperately. His body called to
hers, and hers answered. He made a new song sing inside
her, made her heart labor, ringing like a tolling bell. Every
time he touched her, she wanted to move closer against his
body, to merge with it. She knew she felt that way because
she loved him. Something in his complex spirit called to her
own.

She found herself almost breathless with pleasure and she
cradled his dark head against her velvety flesh, as his lips
and tongue seemed to wrap one rosy peak, then the other
in silken skeins of flame.

With a boldness that surprised her, she pushed his sweater
up so her hands could feel the smooth steely muscles of his
back, his wide chest. He gave a groan of pleasure and, releasing her, ripped the sweater off, flinging it to the floor. He
settled back against the satiny pillows, tasting her mouth,
plundering its secrets as his hands gently cherished her

breasts, making them bloom, straining within his touch. Then his lips supplanted his hands, his lean fingers pressing against her waist to bring her more intimately against the sweet explorations of his mouth, the bathing fire of his tongue.

She gasped, enraptured by his touch, feeling she was turning into liquid, a fountain of fresh desire at which he drank, and yet of which he was the deep and inexhaustible source.

He sighed, nearly panting, and sat up against the pillow, drawing her up with him, his hands on her upper arms, his black eyes devouring her bare shoulders, her small perfect breasts.

"See," he demanded, his gaze moving to her eyes. "You do want me. You're so incredibly beautiful, Perdy. The most beautiful thing I've ever seen in my life. And I want you more than I've ever wanted any woman. And you want me, too. Say it." His dark head bent closer, kissing the space between her breasts. "Say it," he whispered, leaning back and staring into her eyes.

She looked into the depths of that dark gaze, nearly hypnotized. She took in all of him: the blackness of his hair, the perfect straightness of his black brows, his sculpted cheekbones, his fine mouth. She looked at the strong tendons on his neck, the breadth of his golden shoulders, the dark hair like a fine fleece on his chest.

She felt light-headed, giddy, dazzled. Strangely, she did not feel at all self-conscious that she sat there, half-naked, her gown about her waist, her hands on his hard biceps. It seemed the most natural thing in the world.

"Yes," she said, her breath uneven. "I want you, too."

Smiling, he drew her down to him. "I'll take excellent care of you, darling," he said, cynical pleasure in his low voice. "This is going to be a very pleasant arrangement. Beneficial to both of us. I really have the feeling you're going to be the best investment I ever made."

Arrangement. Investment. His words jolted her, chilling her heated body.

She loved him, and she had been ready to give him everything. She had forgotten, momentarily, that he didn't love her, never would love her, and that he wanted only to purchase her for a while. He might just as cavalierly lease a car that took his fancy, but had no intention of keeping.

"You don't love me at all, do you?" she asked, suddenly rigid, now feeling very naked.

The familiar coldness settled on his face. "Of course not. And I never will. What's love got to do with it? I want you. Isn't that enough?"

She pushed away from him, scrambling from the bed. She blushed angrily as she drew her gown back onto her shoulders, and with shaking fingers she fumbled to redo its buttons.

"What the hell's wrong with you?" he demanded, sitting up straight. "Don't act like a child. I'm being honest with you. I want you, I'll take care of you. Now come back here. Don't be a sentimental fool. We both know life's too tough for that."

She could barely make out his features from this distance and she was glad; she was filled with loathing for both him and herself.

"Perdy! You said you wanted me—and I know you do. So stop acting like an idiot. Sex is a normal, healthy urge—"

She managed the last and highest button. She was still breathing hard. "I said I wanted you," she said between gritted teeth. "And once, when I was little, I wanted a bottle of something in the medicine cabinet. It was beautiful and green. It looked delicious. So I drank it. It was poison. They had to send me to the hospital to get my stomach pumped."

She started to stamp barefoot from his bedroom. He leaped up from the bed, towering over her. "And what's that little fable supposed to mean?" he demanded.

"That you're poison, Ben Squires. Pretty poison. And poisoning myself once is enough."

She wrenched her arm away and fled into her bedroom, almost catching the billows of her skirt when she slammed the door.

She rummaged through her closet for clothes, trying to ignore his banging on the door. "Open up!" he commanded. "Open this door and talk to me. I want you. You want me. Let's not ruin it all by dragging love into it, for God's sake. Grow up!"

Mustering all her strength, Perdy put her arms against the chest of drawers and shoved it in front of the door.

"Stay away from me, you snake!" she commanded back. "Don't ever try to touch me again. I don't know how you got the way you are, and I don't care. I don't know what happened to your wife, but whatever it was, I hope it hurt you plenty, because you deserve everything bad that happens to you. No wonder you hate Christmas—it's a season of love; and who could love you?"

There was palpable and ominous silence from the other side of the door. She could imagine him there, tall, barechested, his face hardening like a stone.

Then she heard him walk away. A few moments later, as she hurriedly dressed in jade-green tights and a matching smock with a wide sash, she heard him slam the front door. Then the BMW's motor gunned cruelly, and she heard the roar of its tires as he backed, full speed, out of the driveway.

He didn't come back all afternoon, and she was glad. The garage called, saying her van was ready; she was grateful for that as well. The house seemed empty without him, and she cursed herself for missing him. She felt dazed and emotionally drained. She no longer even had the dream of Cloverdale to console her. He had destroyed that with utter finality.

THE LOUNGE CLOSED EARLY because it was Christmas Eve. She drove home, over the curving mountainous roads, glad to escape Manchester with its Christmas decorations and the carolers singing in the park. She wasn't in the mood for Christmas.

She tried the radio, to distract herself, but the same carols kept nagging at her.

Driving through Mortimerford, she was depressed by the strings of lights ornamenting the library, the illuminated plastic Santa attached to the roof. She was depressed by the nativity scene in front of the courthouse, and by the houses whose windows gleamed with candles and glimpses of lighted Christmas trees.

The house was completely dark when she drove up. She didn't see Ben's car in the drive.

She unlocked the door, kicked off her boots, and trudged into the living room, hanging her cape and hat on the newel post. Bummer, who was still convalescing, padded toward her from his rug and gave her hand a friendly nuzzle.

She patted him and without turning on the lights, walked to the bay window and stared out. A full moon shone behind the mountain, imparting a spectral loveliness, almost a delicacy.

She wondered where Ben was, and if he'd be coming home at all. Coming home, she reflected unhappily—how odd to think of this as his home. She stared at the mountain, wondering what secret it held for him, what he had come back in quest of.

She felt sick with emptiness and doubt. Had she made the right decision?

Her wounded pride voted yes, but the emptiness and longing she felt made her doubtful.

She wandered to the piano, staring down at the black and white keys illuminated by the moonlight, remembering his hands moving across them. She remembered his bruised hand, remembered holding it to her cheek. She remembered his hands more than once on her bare flesh, and how she had loved the feel of them, of him.

She looked up at the ceiling as if she could see through it to the canopy of stars overhead.

"Merry Christmas, Daddy," she whispered. "Merry Christmas, Frankie. Esmeralda. Merry Christmas. I suppose they do it really big, up there."

She shook her head. So much for her Christmas greetings to everyone who loved her. She wasn't going to think about that.

She stretched her slender hand toward the piano and began to play a tune, a carol, the one that haunted her most.

Then, in accompaniment to her halting playing, she sang in her clear contralto:

What child is this
who laid to rest
on Mary's lap is sleeping?
Whom angels greet with anthems sweet—

"Don't." She felt a hand grip her wrist tightly, pull her fingers away from the keys. "Don't, Perdy, not that." She backed away, startled, and he released her immediately. Her heart pounded wildly, with both the shock of fright and the perverse pleasure that he was there.

"Don't," he repeated. There was something strange in his deep voice, and she smelled scotch on his breath. He'd been drinking, she thought with disturbed recognition.

"Where were you?" she demanded, hoping she could hide her agitation at his sudden appearance, at his touch.

"On the couch. Just sitting."

"In the dark?"

He had turned his back on her. He was staring out at the mountain. "Yes, in darkness. The person sitting in darkness."

"Well, I'm putting some light on the subject," she murmured, her heart still thudding. "Where's your car? I didn't see it. You startled me."

She moved to switch on a lamp.

"Don't," he said again, but she did, then slowly turned to look at him.

He gave her a glance over his wide shoulder. His face looked haggard, pale beneath its tan. She picked up the Scotch bottle from the floor beside the couch. It was nearly empty. The last time she'd seen it, it had hardly been touched.

"You've been hitting this stuff a little hard, haven't you?" she asked, trying to sound unconcerned.

He turned to face her, his hands thrust into the pockets of his jeans. "It's all right," he said. "I only do it once a year. On Christmas Eve."

"Nice that you have some sort of tradition," she answered coolly. "And that you have the brains to stay home and not to drive." She could have bitten her tongue for saying "home".

He studied her, watching her carefully. "I am driving. I'm leaving. I just came back for a few things."

The pounding in her heart stopped. It seemed as if her heart had ceased beating altogether. "You shouldn't drive," she objected. "You'd better stay here."

He stared at her intently from beneath his straight, black brows. "I'm leaving. Don't worry. I'm still buying the house. I won't come back until you've moved out. I'm setting you free."

She stared at him in disbelief. She was not sure she wanted to be set free. She opened her mouth but could say nothing.

"Just promise me you won't buy that shop in Cloverdale. That's a mistake I can help you not to make. I can save you from that, at least."

"I—I don't understand this," she stammered. Cloverdale seemed like a misty dream of long ago—insubstantial, unimportant. The only important thing was the troubled man who stood before her.

He shrugged moodily. The lines beside his mouth seemed deeper. "What's to understand? I'm letting you off the hook. Forget about the gore area. I'll buy the property the way it is, clear the problem up myself. You've learned your little lesson in business, I hope. And I'll move out until you can settle elsewhere."

She sank down on the couch. "I don't understand," she repeated numbly.

He gave one of his short, derisive barks of laughter. "I'm tired of you, Perdy. I'm bored of the game. You're too inexperienced for me."

She felt a terrible coldness, a shriveling within her. "Good," she said shakily. "I'm tired of you, too."

He stared at her, his eyes unreadable. He laughed again. "You're a liar. So am I."

She looked up at him. A series of complex emotions played over his face. Her feelings seemed to be wheeling round inside, crashing into each other like a pack of crazed clowns.

He sighed with great weariness. "I'm not tired of you, Perdy. I'm tired of me. I'm tired of being a bastard who can't love anybody. So I'm setting you free. Before it's too late for you."

It was already too late for her, she thought. She didn't want to be free. She couldn't be free if she wanted to. She belonged to him. She always had, she always would. Without any business arrangement, without any contract, without any agreements.

He strolled in front of the empty fireplace, his hands stil
in his pockets, and leaned his back against the mantel.

"I told you the truth when I said I wouldn't marr
again." He gazed back out the window at the mountain
"And I never can love anybody again. I'm incapable of it
But you are capable of love. I think you're even capable o
loving me. That's another mistake I'm going to save you
from making."

"What makes you think I could ever love you?" she par
ried coldly. She felt the old desire to hurt him as much a
he'd hurt her.

"The look on your face this morning. The look on you
beautiful, naked face. The fact you've deeply and trul
loved those whom shallower people might only be unkin
to. The fact that you don't want to be bought; you want t
be loved for yourself. But I don't love. Sometimes I want
But I never love. Not any more. Do you understand that?"

She nodded calmly, as if she didn't care.

"I was up on that mountain ten years ago," he said in
low voice. He nodded at the mountain, silvery in the win
dow. "My Uncle Ben had gone to Florida. I was waitin
there for Sharon—my wife. Things weren't going well be
tween us. We were going to try to make them work. Spen
a Christmas up there, have a tryst, a secret rendezvous o
Miracle Mountain—nobody knowing where we were.
long Christmas of lovemaking. And talking. And getting t
know each other again. To be the way we once had been."

His words jolted her. Sharon—that was the name he ha
muttered in his troubled sleep. Not Cheryl, his sister. Sha
on, his wife. She watched him, wondering how much the li
quor had affected him, wondering what was going o
behind that handsome, stony face.

"She was supposed to join me on Christmas Eve. She'
been off at her aunt's, in Vermont. I had the tree up. Th
champagne iced. Her presents wrapped. Sharon loved pres

ents, especially expensive ones. She would have loved the ones I'd picked."

Perdy was growing concerned for him. He seemed to be sinking deeper into his dark thoughts with each word.

He smiled crookedly, but his eyes looked haunted. "She never came. She was dead."

His wife, she thought helplessly. He'd lost his wife at Christmastime, and he'd been grieving for her ten long years. He had loved someone too much, and he would never love again.

"I'm sorry," she said helplessly.

"I'm not." He laughed. He leaned over and picked up the Scotch bottle. He poured a large dollop into a glass. She watched him with alarm.

"Yes. I am sorry. I can't tell you how sorry," he said, his mouth still crooked, his smile gone. "You accused me last night of laughing at your family, Perdy. I never meant to. I have to admire them. Look what they created—you. And look what my fine family produced—me. Scrooge, you called me. You were right."

He took a long sip of Scotch. "Now my family is something to contemplate. People don't know what happened to Sharon—not really. Money buys such wonderful things— even protection from the truth. None of the family wanted to face the facts—or could bear to have them publicized—so they bought the truth."

"Ben, I don't think you should drink any more—"

He drank again, as if to mock her. "And the truth is that my wife died in my brother's arms. They were lovers. She wasn't in Vermont. And Christopher wasn't on the business trip he was supposed to be on. They were together. Up in Maine, in a ski cabin. And they died together there."

She felt a wave of nauseated horror wash through her. She watched, frightened, as he took the bottle and emptied the remaining Scotch into his glass.

"A space heater malfunctioned in their bedroom." He smiled grimly, and held out his glass as if toasting her. "They died painlessly, in their sleep, of carbon monoxide poisoning. They were naked, of course. Which is not the sort of story a family like mine cares to have circulated."

He threw back his head, took another stiff drink. "So we circulated a different story. With a lot of lying and a lot of money, we made certain the truth never got out. I think it would have killed my mother. She did have a nervous breakdown over it—over the possibility of the loss of our cherished reputation. My sisters, except for little Cheryl, were appalled, not by the deaths, but by the threat that scandal might touch their spotless hems."

He studied his glass, his mouth taut. "So the papers reported that the three of us—Sharon, Christopher, and I were up in Maine together, on a ski holiday; that the heater in the main room malfunctioned—not in the bedroom; and that Sharon and Christopher died tragic and respectable deaths while I spent a long afternoon on the slopes. On the beautiful, glistening slopes.

"So you see, Perdy, it's I who am a freak, not you. You came from a background where people loved each other, in spite of anything. I was the dark sheep who, to save the family pride, has never uttered a word against my dead brother—the extraordinarily charming and reckless Christopher. Nor against my dear, departed wife—the faithful Sharon."

She wanted to rise and go to him, to put her arms around him, but something dark and dangerous in his eyes kept her frozen.

"And then you took over Toynbee's?" she whispered.

He sipped deeply at his drink. "Ah, yes. To straighten out the mess Christopher had created. Somebody had to. More than the family welfare depended on it. Toynbee's is a large enterprise. It affects thousands. Pulling it back together was almost a relief. Maybe it kept me sane. That, and my silly little sister, who in spite of everything, is truly fond of me.''

He held his glass out toward her again, another parody of a toast. "But even Cheryl doesn't know the most ironic part. She was too young then to be told. And nobody in the family has spoken of it since. They've all come to believe the lie they created. They actually have. They've lived the lie so long it's real to them. But the truth is that Sharon and Christopher had been lovers for some time. And why shouldn't he have beguiled her? The earnest young medical student was amusing for a while, but Christopher was the charmer, the holder of the power.''

He took another drink. "So the most ironic part is that the autopsy showed Sharon was pregnant. It would have been a little girl. And to my dying day, I'll never know if that child—that innocent child—was mine or my brother's. That gives me something to think of every Christmas. Cheers.''

He tossed the last of the Scotch down easily, set the glass on the mantel, and leaned against the wall, his face twisted with bitter memories.

Perdy sat, her hands clenched tightly together in her lap. She watched him. A muscle worked in his jaw. A vein leaped in his temple. He suddenly looked too distant for her to reach. He looked as closed and alien as a man who had come from another star. She knew, instinctively, it was the child he was thinking of.

She ached for him. She could think of nothing to say nor did she want to say anything. She wanted only to go to him, to put her arms around him, lean her face against his chest and feel the beat of his heart. She wanted him to put his arms around her, too, and for even a little while, forget the past. She would stay in his arms, as long as he wanted, under any terms he set.

"Don't look at me that way," he said, his voice low, husky.

Confusion swarmed through her. "What way? I don't know what you mean..."

"That way," he said with a curt nod, his eyes not meeting hers. "As if you'd tear out your heart and hand it to me if I wanted it. Just remember you were right. I'm poison. And I'm poisoned. Through and through. You deserve better. You deserve more, and there's no chance you'll ever get it from me."

He straightened. He made his way to the hall closet, his gait still even. He put on his parka. He slipped on his gloves with that same careless, elegant gesture she had noticed the first night.

"We won't see each other again," he said matter-of-factly. "Algie and Puckett can work out the details on the house. I'll make sure it's fast."

She stood up, her hands falling helplessly to her sides. "Don't go," she said.

"I can drive," he replied, casting a glance out the window at the mountain. "I'm not drunk yet. Not nearly as drunk as I intend to get. So long. I won't wish you a Merry Christmas. I've rather guaranteed you won't have that. So, I trust, if nothing else, you've learned a valuable lesson from this—always be careful about what you sign. Take care, Perdy. Take good care."

He was already at the door. "Ben, don't go! Please! And don't drive!"

But as if he didn't hear her, he left, closing the door behind him. She raced out following him. She forgot she had on neither hat nor coat, and that except for her tights, she was barefoot.

His car was parked under the pines, half-hidden. She floundered toward it, tumbling through the snow.

"Ben! Please don't go!" she cried out again. The snow burned her feet like fire. "Please!"

He was already in his car. He started it and backed away swiftly, clouds of snow churning up from under his wheels.

She stood watching until his headlights disappeared. Then she was alone, still watching. In the distance, the mountain where once he had been happy, where once he had kissed her, loomed silver, silent, pitiless, a mass of ice and stone. The moonlight shone behind it, like a halo. In the distance, in the village, church bells rang because it was midnight. It was Christmas.

"Ben," she whispered to the cold air. "Forgive them. And forgive yourself."

She sank to her knees in the snow and wept, not for herself, but for him.

CHAPTER TEN

SHE HAD SPENT AN UNEASY NIGHT on the couch, unable to bear even the thought of sleeping alone in her bed or his. She had taken the coverlet from his bed, though, as if lying beneath it would somehow bring him closer.

Her dreams had been frightening ones: Ben alone, his car going too fast, skidding on the winding, icy roads and crashing.

She had relived the terrible taunts she had made to him about Christmas, knowing, this time, how deeply her words must have stabbed him.

In and out of her dreams had drifted the crying of a faceless child, an infant who was lost and seeking someone.

She rose, dressed, and for the first time since Nels's funeral, went to church. She put on no makeup except a touch of lip gloss. It was the kind of day that she needed to meet with an honest and naked face. She had become weary of masks, of hiding her true self from the world. From now on, the world would have to take her as she was.

She drove into Manchester, to Esmeralda's former church. Like the old mill buildings that lined the river in Manchester, the exterior was red and weathered brick, pocked with soot. But within, it was as lovely a church as she had ever seen.

The wall behind the altar was a beautiful tracery of delicate white filigree and sculpture that rose, arched and ornate, to the vaulted ceiling.

The stained-glass windows were tall and narrow, and she wondered if the church had been built by the French mill workers. The service itself was in French, and she understood nothing.

Although she was not religious, she had attended church with Esmeralda often enough to be familiar with the rituals. After the service, she stopped and lit candles for Nels, for Frankie, and for Esmeralda. She looked at all the votive lights, gleaming in their jewel-like containers, then lit one more for Ben.

She drove home through the snowy streets slowly. The city was quiet, the madness of Christmas shopping over. The village, too, was peaceful. A few children played on snowy lawns with new sleds or snowshoes. A pair of cross-country skiers glided, laughing, down a side street.

At home, she changed into her jeans, mukluks, and a white cotton turtleneck pullover. She donned a tattered sweater made of all the colors of the rainbow, which Esmeralda had knitted for her one Christmas many years before.

She took Bummer for a long walk. He seemed fully recovered but skirted the edge of the pond warily.

She walked to the edge of the mountain, then down to the brook, which winter had sculpted into designs as elaborate and beautiful as those behind the altar of the church.

She went back to the empty house. Bummer was reluctant to go inside. He had a lot of rambling to catch up on. Perdy watched through the glass doors as he bounded to the edge of the woods, then disappeared into its darkness.

"So you're leaving, too," she thought glumly, then scolded herself for groveling in self-pity. She heated up a prepared dinner she found in the freezer. It was tasteless.

She went into the living room, and feeling furtive like an intruder, went through Ben's record albums and put a Gilbert and Sullivan on the stereo. She snuggled up on the couch and tried to read. She could not concentrate.

All right, she lectured herself. He doesn't love you, can't love you, will never love you. At least he was honest enough to tell the truth. How could he love anybody again? In one devastating day, he had lost his wife, his brother, perhaps his child. In the season of love, he had been betrayed by those who should have been closest to him. He had lost his faith in people, family, love.

He had given up his career, devoted himself to saving the failing fortunes of a family who betrayed him. He had lived a lie for ten years, to protect the reputations of the very people who had nearly shattered his life. How could he love again? Even if he did, why should he love her, of all people?

She tried to think of what she was going to do and could not. She couldn't think about Cloverdale at all. How silly and childish it seemed to her now, to have to pretend a place was home. Home wasn't a place; home was people. Home was someone she had yet to find. No. Home was someone she had found briefly, then lost.

She could not think about that either. All her thoughts orbited like planets around a tall man with wide shoulders, no hips, and a face so lean and handsome.

Perdy was startled when the phone rang. It was Algie.

"Ben's doing this against my advice," he said pettishly. "You should be responsible for that gore area. But at least he's getting you out of there, and I intend to see it's done as quickly as possible. I intend to pull strings. I intend to close this deal so fast your head will spin."

He set her teeth on edge. "Don't you ever take a day off, Algie? It's Christmas, you know."

"Don't you dare call me Algie," he snorted. "Don't you dare be familiar with me. I'm an attorney. And I'm thankful Ben's got you out of his system at last. You're not our kind."

His words scalded, but sent her fighting spirit coursing through her blood. "I'm glad I'm not your kind Algie. Goodbye!"

"Don't you hang up on me," he ordered. "I want to warn you. Don't think you're getting anything other than the sale of the house out of this little escapade. Don't you come around trying to blackmail this family because you happen to be another of Ben's little indiscretions. Of all the women he's ever picked to smirch the name of my sainted sister, you are the worst."

Perdy's mind pounced on his statement like a cat on a mouse. "What's your sainted sister have to do with this?" she demanded, feeling that she already knew.

"My dear half-sister was Ben's wife. And she was everything that you are not. So be forewarned that once this sale is closed, I don't want to hear any more out of you."

His hypocrisy sickened her. "I understand perfectly," she returned. "And one of the things I understand is that if Ben didn't keep you on his payroll, you'd starve to death!"

She slammed the phone down with such a crash that it hurt her ears.

Then she sat on the floor, drew up her knees and pressed her face against them. Poor Ben, she thought miserably. Algie was his brother-in-law and part of the continuing charade of the faithful wife and the loving brother Christopher.

Part of her was wounded by Algernon's words. It bothered her that he said she wasn't "their kind," that she was merely another one of Ben's "indiscretions."

Oh, she thought, wearily, *I can't think about this any longer. I'll drive myself mad.* But she couldn't help thinking of it. She felt sick with grief and longing and loss.

By four o'clock in the afternoon, she could stand the loneliness no more. She decided she would go to the movies. After she'd seen one, she'd go see another, then another, and then another, until she could stay awake just long enough to drive home.

She was sitting on her bed, struggling with the zipper on one of her good boots and ready to weep. The last time it had stuck, Ben had been there to fix it. Then she heard a loud vehicle pull up outside. It sounded like a truck of some sort.

"Ugh!" she muttered, managing to unjam the zipper of the boot. She went downstairs into the living room and looked out the bay window. A massive green truck with a gold logo she didn't recognize was parked in the drive and two burly men trudged toward her door, each carrying two large vases loaded with white roses. Each bundle was wrapped in clear paper to protect the flowers from the cold.

She stood, leaning on the windowsill, staring in disbelief. Roses being delivered—and in vases? The bell rang, and she ran to answer it. "What is this?" she asked the two men. She could barely see them through the roses.

"Don't ask me, lady. I just take orders," one rasped.

Without another word they passed her, looked around the room, and silently began setting the vases on the living-room floor.

"Just what's going on here?" she demanded again, her hands on her hips. "Why are you putting them on the floor?"

"Lady," said one of the men, "we're puttin' 'em on the floor because we gotta. There's more."

Her brown eyes blinked, hard. "What?"

But they lapsed into silence and trudged back out the door. In a few moments they returned with more roses.

"Look," she said desperately. "There's some mistake here! Take these back out."

"No mistake," the deliveryman replied laconically. "This is a special order—very special—from the top."

The roses were taking over the living room by now, but the two men went outside again and returned with more.

"Listen," she said, trying to stop them. "You can't have the right house. There are no cards on these or anything—somebody down the road must be getting married or something. Hey! Why the kitchen floor? What's wrong with the table?"

"There's more," the man said tonelessly.

"Well, how many more?" she pleaded, staring at the engulfing sea of flowers.

"Altogether—" frowned the man, "—a thousand. It ain't easy gettin' a thousand roses on a holiday, then getting them all packed up in vases—then finding a way to deliver them safely. Somebody did a lot of callin' around. By the way, you've gotta fill these things with water."

"A thousand roses!" she cried. Would ridiculous things never cease happening to her? Ever since she'd set foot in New Hampshire, her life had been a series of upheavals, great and small.

The men continued lugging the roses in—all white. They covered most of the living-room floor, the piano, the occasional tables, the kitchen floor, the kitchen table, and all the counter space.

"Stop!" she begged them. "There's no more room. Go back!"

"This house got bedrooms?" the man asked. She nodded numbly. "Then you got more room," he said logically.

She snatched up her jacket and ran outside to look at the truck more closely. The gold letters on the logo spelled out Toynbee's in curling script.

Toynbee's, she thought wildly, rushing back inside. The roses must belong to Ben. He must have ordered them for a housewarming party or something—and someone, somewhere, had got the date of delivery wrong.

"Listen," she pleaded, seizing the shorter man by the sleeve of his jacket. "Are these roses for Mr. Squires? Because if they are—you have the wrong day. He doesn't live here yet."

The man stared down at her hand clutching his sleeve, then up at her. "It's the right date," he said defensively. "We're gettin' paid double overtime and a bonus for workin' today. And the flowers ain't for Mr. Squires. They're *from* Mr. Squires. Now let go, lady. I got about twenty dozen more roses out there."

Well, she said to herself, I have actually done it. I have actually gone mad. Insanity wasn't so bad after all. At least it smelled good.

Perdy went back into the living room and watched the men carrying in roses, feeling like the hapless sorcerer's apprentice who could not stem the flood once it had started.

"That's it," the man finally said. He tipped his cap. "Merry Christmas, lady."

He and his partner disappeared out the door.

"What am I going to do?" she cried aloud, listening to the truck pull away. "It looks like somebody died here!"

"No," said a familiar low voice. "Just the opposite. Somebody came back to life."

She turned around. Ben Squires stood in the open doorway, his height nearly filling it. He stared at her, his black eyes studying her carefully, as if she were an apparition that might disappear.

She walked slowly toward him, studying him in exactly the same way. She wanted to be sure he was real.

In one arm he held a Christmas tree decorated with feathery white doves and red silken hearts. In the other he held a strange bare tree that looked quite dead and had an odd roundish plastic package fastened to it on a naked bow.

She looked at him, her heart leaping like a dear. "What are you doing?" she asked softly, not quite believing he was really there. "Are you all right? What are you doing with that?" She pointed at the Christmas tree.

He looked slightly embarrassed. "A Christmas tree," he said. "I thought you ought to have a proper one."

"Then what on earth is that?" She pointed to the other leafless tree, its roots trussed up in a bag.

He shrugged. "Er—it's a pear tree. Very hard to find a pear tree at this time of year."

"A pear tree? Ben, have you gone mad? Or have I? What's that thing tied onto its branch?"

He did look embarrassed. "It's a frozen duck. I bought it at the supermarket. I couldn't find a partridge."

Her hands flew to her face in a gesture of embarrassment. "You what? Duck—partridge—why?"

He shrugged again, not taking his eyes from hers. "I wanted to bring you a partridge in a pear tree. Like in the song: 'On the first day of Christmas my true love gave to me—a partridge in a pear tree.' All I could get was this stupid duck. Sorry."

Her heart was still leaping as if it would fly out of her chest and go soaring over the mountain. He was back. He was really back. "Why did you want to give me a partridge in a pear tree?"

"Because." He looked down at her, his dark eyes serious. "Because it's the first day of Christmas. And you're my true love. At least, oh, I hope you will be. Will you, Perdy?"

She swallowed, hard. She couldn't say anything, but her eyes told him what he needed to know.

He leaned both trees against the wall, bent down and wrapped her in his strong arms. "So ask me inside, will you? Because I love you. And I want to marry you. And, like a fool, I nearly lost you."

The fur of his parka tickled her nose. He needed a shave; the stubble of his jaw burned against her cheek. She didn't mind at all. If she was dreaming, she didn't want to wake up. Had he actually said he wanted to marry her?

"I don't think there's room for your trees inside," she laughed, her arms going around his neck. "It's full of roses."

"Ah. Yes. Well. That." Chagrin was in his deep voice. His breath tickled her ear. "Yes. Well. I'll explain that."

He took her hand and led her into the living room. He paused, gritted his teeth, and frowned. "Yes. Well. It is a lot of roses, isn't it? Come on."

He led her to the couch and sat, pulling her down into his lap, his arms around her. He kissed her throat.

"What's happened to you?" she asked, half laughing, half crying, pressing her face against his shoulder.

He kissed the nape of her neck. "Scrooge got converted, darling. All night long the ghosts of Christmas chased me around. They're very convincing fellows, those ghosts."

"What do you mean? I don't understand you." She drew back to look into his face. He was grinning ironically at her, his black eyes full of life.

He pulled her back against him. "Don't go so far away," he murmured against her hair. He threaded his fingers through her dark brown locks and kissed the tip of her ear. "Listen. I got drunk last night, and it didn't do me a bit of good. The drunker I got, the more I thought of you. And the next thing I knew, I was sitting in church."

"Church?" She snuggled more closely against his chest. "You? The big cynic?"

"Look, darling," he said, kissing her ear again. "I don't know why. I was just there, and all I could think about was you."

She tried to ease away slightly, to look up at his face. But he refused to release her, held her tighter still. "It finally hit me, Perdy, that for ten years I'd let the past embitter and haunt me. Then you came along, a paradox of fire and ice, tough and sweet, sharp and soft. You'd driven away the ghost of Christmas past—at long last. He couldn't stand up against a girl like you."

His arms tightened around her. His lips were warm against her ear. "And I knew then that not only had I lied to you last night, I'd lied to myself. I said I couldn't love ou—but I already did. I was too much a fool to admit it until I walked away. I think I loved you from the first night, when you opened the door, your head so high that I knew Algie would never be a match for you. In fact, you might never meet your match—unless it was going to be me. I loved you. I do love you. I'll always love you."

He pressed his lips against her hair, his breathing as ragged as on the night outside the lounge when he had held her so tightly. "I always knew I wanted you. I was too twisted by the past to confess even to myself that I loved you. But when I left you here last night, I didn't leave you at all. You were in my mind, in my blood. You haunted me. You became my Ghost of Christmas Present."

His hands framed her face, drawing her back so he could look at her. He smiled the tight-lipped smile she'd learned to love. "But what put me over the edge was the Ghost of Christmas Future—of any future without you. Because you're gallant and sweet and funny and honest and beautiful, even in the morning with no makeup and your big glasses. You couldn't have cared less about my money or my power or my family name. You cared for right and wrong and fighting for what you believed in. Yet, somehow, I felt you came to care for me. So don't go out of my future—marry me. Now. Today."

She wound her arms around his neck, kissing him deeply. "Yes. Yes," she whispered against his lips. "Yes, yes, yes, I love you, too." She drew back a bit, her eyes shining. "But, Ben—why did you send all these roses?"

His smile was endearingly embarrassed. He licked his lips. "Well . . . I said some horrible things to you last night. I figured a dozen roses would never say how sorry I was. So I sent a thousand. I was still a little drunk when I thought that up. I called my secretary, and I believe I rashly promised her two weeks in Bermuda if she could pull it off."

She shook her head fondly, smiling up at him. "Why didn't you come back sooner? I was miserable without you."

He kissed the tip of her nose. "I was busy. I drove to Toynbee's, opened it up, and picked out the biggest diamond ring we had. I had to check on a state where we could get married tonight. It's Rhode Island. I had to charter a plane to fly us. I had to get your Christmas tree. And your pear tree. And your duck."

"It's a very nice duck," she said, smiling. "It's the nicest duck anybody ever gave me."

"Then put him in the freezer, Perdy," Ben ordered, brushing his fingers against her cheek. "And don't bother to pack. We'll fly back here tonight. I can't think of a better place for a honeymoon. So let's announce our engagement, then you can change clothes and we'll drive to the airport."

"Who are we announcing our engagement to?" she asked, laughing. "The trees? The duck?"

"Well, I've already told Cheryl, who's delighted. Who does that leave that we're closest to?" he asked in return. "To the dog, of course. He's practically family."

He swung her up into his arms and made his way through all the roses to the kitchen. He opened the sliding glass doors and carried her onto the deck.

"Give that whistle of yours," he said.

She put two fingers to her mouth and gave two short whistles. In a moment, Bummer came bounding out of the woods, then ran in circles, waiting for them to come down for a walk.

"Bummer!" Ben yelled. "It's us! We're going to make it legal. We wanted you to be among the first to know—congratulate us!"

Bummer paused, eyeing them curiously, then raised his hind leg and dampened a small evergreen.

Ben frowned, then looked down at her. "He doesn't seem impressed. I hate a cynic. Don't you?"

"Yes," she agreed. "But don't worry. We'll straighten him out."

He grinned, then kissed her. "Listen, Perdy, do you know what this means? We're going to have very tall children."

She nodded. "They'll be dark, too."

"With long legs," he added.

"And deep voices," she said.

"And," he reminded her, "we have this very tall dog, a dark one, with long legs and a deep voice."

"I like it," she said happily. "We'll all match."

"Perfectly," he said, and kissed her. "Do you want to see your ring?"

"Later," she breathed. "First kiss me some more."

He did, and very thoroughly.

"Perdy," Esmeralda had always said, "I have the feeling that one of these days you're going to find a heck of a man. Just one heck of a man."

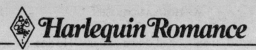 **Harlequin Romance**

Coming Next Month

2809 THE TULLAGINDI RODEO Kerry Allyne
What's a rich girl to do when the Australian bush guide she
falls in love with thinks she's a spoiled brat? Why, get what
she wants, of course, and let him see the woman she
really is.

2810 RIDE A WILD HORSE Jane Donnelly
Twenty-two years old and longing for adventure. But it's
foolhardy for a young woman to fall for the wildly
confident organizer of an archaeological dig near her
Cotswold village if he'll only be around for the summer.

2811 SWEET PRETENDER Virginia Hart
Reluctantly, a young vacationer goes along with her sister's
masquerading as the daughter of a former Connecticut
resident. But she regrets her complicity when the pretense
stands in the way of her love.

2812 NEVER TOUCH A TIGER Sue Peters
A trapeze artist's life swings upside down when she comes
up against an arrogant English lord who threatens her
uncle's circus—not to mention her heart.

2813 UNLIKELY LOVERS Emily Spenser
A graduating botany student knows her idol has had his fill
of adoring young students. Still, she sets out to win his
respect in the hope that one day he'll make room in his
life for love.

2814 PERFUMES OF ARABIA Sara Wood
Normally, this English schoolteacher hates men like Tarik—
masterful, dynamic and ruthless. But his desert country
mesmerizes her with its timeless magic—as does the man.

Available in January wherever paperback books are sold, or
through Harlequin Reader Service.

In the U.S.
P.O. Box 1397
Buffalo, N.Y.
14240-1397

In Canada
P.O. Box 603
Fort Erie, Ontario
L2A 9Z9

Take 4 novels and a surprise gift FREE

Take 4 novels and a surprise gift FREE

Janet Dailey
Americana

Don't miss a single title from this great collection. The first eight titles have already been published. Complete and mail this coupon today to order books you may have missed.

Harlequin Reader Service

In U.S.A.
901 Fuhrmann Blvd.
P.O. Box 1397
Buffalo, N.Y. 14140

In Canada
P.O. Box 2800
Postal Station A
5170 Yonge Street
Willowdale, Ont. M2N 6J3

Please send me the following titles from the Janet Dailey Americana Collection. I am enclosing a check or money order for $2.75 for each book ordered, plus 75¢ for postage and handling.

_____	ALABAMA	Dangerous Masquerade
_____	ALASKA	Northern Magic
_____	ARIZONA	Sonora Sundown
_____	ARKANSAS	Valley of the Vapours
_____	CALIFORNIA	Fire and Ice
_____	COLORADO	After the Storm
_____	CONNECTICUT	Difficult Decision
_____	DELAWARE	The Matchmakers

Number of titles checked @ $2.75 each = $_____

N.Y. RESIDENTS ADD
    APPROPRIATE SALES TAX $_____

Postage and Handling $____.75___

TOTAL $_____

I enclose _____

(Please send check or money order. We cannot be responsible for cash sent through the mail.)

PLEASE PRINT

NAME _____

ADDRESS _____

CITY _____

STATE/PROV. _____

BLJD-A-1

On Saturday afternoon she is recovering from her breakfast of cereal and banana when her doorbell rings. She thinks it is Subu again, but looking out of her window, she can't see Subu's Audi. She takes off her dressing gown and changes into sweatpants. It is a cold day. She opens the door of her flat and Wale is walking up the stairs.

"What are you doing here?"

"I came to see you."

"Who let you in?"

"Your neighbor. She was on her way out."

She hugs him out of shock, but he doesn't hold her.

"What's wrong?" she asks.

"Can we?" he asks, pointing indoors.

"What for?"

"I want to talk to you."

"About?"

"You want to talk out here?"

She crosses her arms. "It depends what you have to say."

"Paris."

"That's why you came?"

He shuts her door after he walks in and looks around as if he expects to find an orgy.

"I don't know what is going on," he says, "but I have just told my family about you. You don't want to meet them? Fine. You have other men in your life? Fine with me. All I need to know is if you are pregnant or not. I also have the right to know if you have jeopardized my health. Now, I'm sure you have evidence of the tests you've had and I want to see them."

Jeopardize. She is still a little nauseous. She will always associate her love for him with nausea. She goes to her bedroom and retrieves her tests from the drawer by her bed and hands them to him.

"Are you satisfied?" she asks, as he reads.

"What was the phone call I had with that man about?"

"I've known him longer than I've known you."

"You didn't mention you were going to Paris."

Typical, she thinks. The moment he opens up, he is given to acts of heroism, flying across the Sahara to stand on her head and stick a flag in her arse.

"He's gay," she says.